S w e e t m e a t s

---◇◇◇---

We all lust after what we cannot have, from forbidden sweets as a child to forbidden pleasures as an adult. The most dangerous and extraordinary temptations are often the most exciting, the most alluring. What we are forbidden to touch is always what we yearn to feel. The fruit we are forbidden to taste is always sure to be the juiciest. And the higher up that fruit grows, the farther it is out of our reach, the sweeter, riper, and more delicious it is destined to be.

In this collection, four of our favorite authors have provided us with a bountiful collection of stories bursting with desire, lust, and fruity themes. *Forbidden Fruit* offers up a platter of erotic tales for your delectation. Peel back the layers, savor the sweetness, and sate your senses until the juices run down your chin!

A Sweetmeats Book

First published by Sweetmeats Press 2015

Copyright © Sweetmeats Press 2015

All characters in this publication are fictitious and any resemblance to real persons, living or dead, is purely coincidental.

All rights reserved.
No part of this publication may be reproduced, stored in a retrieval system, or transmitted, in any form or by any means, without the prior permission in writing from Sweetmeats Press. Nor may it be circulated in any form of binding or cover other than that in which it is published and without a similar condition, including this condition being imposed on the subsequent purchaser.

ISBN 978-1-909181-61-8

Typeset by Sweetmeats Press
Printed and bound in the U.S.

Sweetmeats Press
27 Old Gloucester Street, London, WC1N 3XX, England, U. K.
www.sweetmeatspress.com

FORBIDDEN FRUIT

compiled by

KOJO BLACK

East Baton Rouge Parish Library
Baton Rouge, Louisiana

"There is a charm about the forbidden that makes it unspeakably desirable."

−Mark Twain (1835 − 1910)

Contents

SUMMER PUDDING
by TAMSIN FLOWERS   7

THE LOVE APPLE
by ZAK JANE KEIR   73

A DANCE OF OCEAN MAGIC
by ELIZABETH BLACK   111

THE CHERRY ORCHARD
by VANESSA DE SADE   155

Summer Pudding

Tamsin Flowers

Summer Pudding

The television studio's green room wasn't green, but his eyes were. So intensely green that they momentarily robbed Lisa Summer of the power of speech.

"I said, *bonjour*." His accent was strong. French, obviously.

"I … sorry … hello."

She'd only just been deposited in the green room by the runner who'd collected her from reception, and she hadn't got her bearings. But she knew who he was, the man with the emerald eyes. He was Laurent Gillou. Owner of Le Petit Pois. Winner of three Michelin stars, three times over. Author of seven best-selling cookbooks. And representative of the heaving over-consumption and food elitism sweeping the country's middle classes. Lisa had analyzed recipes in his books—she had yet to find a dish that carried less than six hundred calories and lashings of saturated fat.

"You are the nutrition expert, *oui*?"

She nodded, holding out a hand. "Lisa Summer."

She expected him to shake her hand, but Laurent Gillou raised it slowly to his mouth and kissed it. His lips lingered on the back of her hand, as his eyes locked with hers.

"You know, you're wrong about food," he said, as he let her hand drop. "But we will see when the debate starts. May the best man win."

"Woman," corrected Lisa. "You'll find that I know what I'm talking about."

Ugh! The man was so arrogant. She turned her back on him and strolled across to the complementary buffet, looking over it with a critical eye. When were caterers going to learn that mini sausage rolls weren't healthy? And who even liked them?

Secretly, however, she was thrilled to be here. She still couldn't believe that she'd been asked onto national television to give her expert opinion on food and nutrition. *Opinions in Opposition* was the country's most popular early evening show. Each week it pitted experts with opposing opinions against each other in what very often turned out to be explosive discussions. Of course, Lisa was fully aware that the show's reptilian host, Dexter Dixon, did all he could to inflame passions on either side, but she felt confident that she could hold her own. She knew her stuff and she'd always had a cool head.

"Perhaps, *mademoiselle*, we share an opinion on the wretchedness of this offering."

She turned to face Gillou so she could study him more closely. In the flesh, he looked vastly different to the man on the cover of his books. Thinner, a little more refined than the ruddy-faced *bon viveur* in a chef's white tunic with the three gold stars on the breast. His dark suit was exquisitely cut, his salt and pepper hair immaculate. But with his aquiline nose and penetrating eyes, his look was defiantly Gallic.

"Perhaps," said Lisa, "but we wouldn't agree on an alternative."

Dexter Dixon hustled into the room and hurried over to them.

"Ah-ha, you two have already met. Splendid. Now, Debs will take you for a bit of pimpage in hair and makeup, then the battle can commence."

Lisa watched Gillou bridle at the suggestion he needed to be pimped in any way, but she would welcome the attentions of the professionals. She wanted to look her best. Her mother would be watching.

An hour later, she felt decidedly unlike herself

with a ferociously tight chignon and a layer of makeup so thick she could barely change her expression. Debs propelled her into the studio as Dexter Dixon began his introduction of her. The lights were blinding. Beyond them, the studio audience was a dark, shadowy mass.

"Lisa Summer is a qualified nutritionist. A woman who certainly knows her goji berries from her chia seeds. Welcome, Lisa."

There was a small ripple of clapping as she took the seat she'd been instructed to go to, then silence.

"And today, our nutritional expert will be butting heads with a man who worships food for its rich flavors, the pleasures it can afford." Dexter paused for effect. "Laurent Gillou needs no introduction ..."

His words were drowned out by a raucous cheer from the audience that continued as Gillou appeared at the studio entrance, and lasted until he'd shaken hands with both Dexter and Lisa. He took his seat, then raised both his palms, then lowered them slowly, conducting the audience to settle down.

"*Merci, merci.*"

Dexter Dixon didn't stand a chance.

Lisa Summer didn't stand a chance.

Laurent Gillou had the viewers eating out of his hand—no one was remotely interested in why they should eat five servings of vegetables a day.

"Let's get this discussion rolling," said Dexter,

raising his voice as the audience caught their breath. "Miss Summer, why don't you start us off? Tell us, why shouldn't we eat whatever we want, what tastes good to us?"

Lisa was prepared. She'd know she'd be faced with the most fatuous of questions from Dexter Dixon.

"Of course, the way food tastes is important," she said.

Laurent Gillou gave an exaggerated nod, turning his head to scan the audience as he did.

Lisa ignored him and continued. "But unfortunately not all foods that taste good are beneficial to your health." The audience emitted a tired sigh. "Luckily, however, you can combine the two—there's nothing as delicious as a fresh, crisp salad with some lean chicken breast or a slice of poached salmon."

Laurent Gillou's bark of laughter encouraged similar snorts from beyond the lights.

"I can think of almost a thousand things more delicious than those," he said.

"All of which will damage your heart and your waistline, no doubt," said Lisa.

Thirty minutes later, neither of them had budged an inch on their respective views.

"The problem, Miss Summer, with people like you," Gillou said, "is that you don't understand the pleasure principle. If something gives you great pleasure, it must be good for you. You derive a value from that aspect of it, over and above the mere calorie and vitamin content."

The audience gasped its approval.

"I don't agree," said Lisa. "It's important …

Gillou cut her off.

"It's like sex. The content is just two bodies rubbing together. But the value? It can be something transcendental, beautiful." A flurry of spontaneous clapping. "Food and sex? These are what makes life bearable on this isolated little rock, where we face only the inevitability of death."

The audience erupted in their agreement.

Lisa's jaw set tight. There was really little she could offer in the face of the inevitability of death.

"Fine words, *Monsieur* Gillou," said Dexter Dixon, once the uproar had died down. "Anything to add? Your final point, Lisa?"

Lisa swallowed. What the hell could she say?

"*Monsieur* Gillou, your transcendental assertions mean nothing to school children who are suffering from malnutrition because it would never cross their parents mind to simply feed them some vegetables."

"I agree, *mademoiselle*. Poverty and ignorance is a tragedy. But perhaps I can offer you a challenge. I'll donate one full week's takings from Le Petis Pois to the nutritional charity of your choice, if you can resist my culinary seduction."

He swept his eyes from one side of the audience to the other, as if he were challenging them. They emitted a collective sigh.

Dexter Dixon turned to Lisa.

"What do you say, Miss Summer. Will you accept Laurent's challenge?"

"What would it involve?" *She should have just said no.*

"You come to Le Petit Pois for two days and allow me to prepare for you a dish so pleasurable that you'll forget all about its nutritional credentials."

"Oh, Miss Summer, please say you will," said Dexter Dixon. His eyes twinkled.

"Yes!" called a man.

"Do it!" shrieked a woman.

"Go for it!" said several voices at once.

The audience wanted the experience vicariously.

Dixon turned to Laurent Gillou. "We could film this, yes?"

Gillou shook his head. "No, my recipes are secret. But I will bring Miss Summer back to the studio to tell you all about it."

Lisa was trapped. There was no way she could refuse. And the steady strumming of a pulse at the base of her throat, combined with a rush of heat between her legs, told her she didn't want to.

"Yes, I'll do it."

Damn! What had she just walked herself into?

Lisa barely stopped to fetch her coat from the green room. She wanted to get out of the TV studio as fast as she possibly could. Now she'd have to come up with some way to wriggle out of this ridiculous commitment. Then, waiting for the elevator, the worst thing happened. Laurent Gillou came and stood beside her.

He cleared his throat.

She ignored him.

"*Mademoiselle* Summer, I have to say, you made some very good points about fresh food and good health."

Lisa's jaw might have come close to hitting the floor.

"Thank you."

"I very much look forward to some more discussion when you come to Le Petit Pois."

"About that …"

"My assistant will telephone you to fix a date. Please give me your number."

The doors opened. Gillou stood back to allow her in first. They stood facing each other across the mirrored box, as Lisa recited her mobile number. In the mirrors, she could see an infinite number of Gillous and a corresponding number of Lisas. A dozen pairs of those sharp green eyes. A dozen pairs of his sensuous lips which, as she watched, curled into a smile.

"Let me warn you, Lisa." He used her first name. "I will win this challenge. I will beguile you with my most exquisite creation."

Was he being serious? She smiled back at him.

"What will you cook for me? How will you tempt me?"

"That I will decide on the day." He stepped forward, until they were less than a foot apart, and Lisa became acutely aware of his scent—vetiver and sandalwood. Heat prickled at the back of her neck. "Something that your beautiful mouth won't be able to resist." As he said this, he reached up to trace the outline of her lips with a fingertip. Lisa reeled, but it was all she could do not to push the tip of her tongue out between her lips.

Jesus! Get a grip!

The doors opened. Gillou strode away without another word.

Gillou's assistant—French, naturally—was efficiency personified. She also appeared to have had a charm bypass. She barked instructions down the phone about how to get to Le Petit Pois, when Lisa was expected and what she should wear. The restaurant was deep in the heart of the countryside and she would be expected to stay the night. So, two solid days with Laurent Gillou. Would that be long enough to re-educate him and win this silly challenge? She'd be damned if she didn't give it her best shot.

"On the first day," continued the assistant, "you'll be spending time in the kitchen, so I recommend casual clothes and comfortable shoes. Then, on your second day with us, Monsieur Gillou would like you to dress appropriately for a meal in our dining room. Our private dining room. *Comprenez-vous?*"

Lisa wasn't sure she did. After all, what was the distinction, in terms of dress, between the public and the private dining room? For no reason at all, she packed her best underwear.

It was already hot by the time Lisa steered her little Citroen through the imposing gates of Le Petit Pois a few minutes after ten o'clock. The officious woman had instructed her to arrive at ten and it hadn't been Lisa's intention to be late. But her old car didn't offer the luxury of sat nav, so she'd had to drive and map-read at the same time. At least they couldn't disapprove of her choice of car.

The gravel drive wound through the most spectacular stands of rhododendron—at least they would have been, if they'd been in flower. But it was

July now, and their blooms were long since over. Still, it made her think of the driveway to Manderley, and her heart beat a little faster with each twist and turn. Finally, the dark cavern of bushes gave way to a thicket of Scotch pines, standing sentinel as the drive curved in a carriage circle. A grand sweep, at the apex of which stood the most perfectly beautiful house Lisa had ever laid eyes on.

Le Petit Pois was a small Tudor manor that had once belonged to the brother or father or uncle of one of Henry the Eighth's wives—Lisa had read about it on the restaurant website, but she couldn't remember the details. Flint stone walls, timber frame above and a forest of spiral brick chimneys stretching up to the sky.

Lisa parked her car to one side of the carriage sweep and got out, staring up at the house. Of course, she'd seen pictures of it online, but nothing had prepared her for its absolute perfection, an architectural concoction of red, black and white against the cobalt sky. She sighed.

"Miss Summer, you found us!"

She tore her eyes from the intricate brickwork of the chimneys to find Laurent Gillou bearing down on her. This time he was dressed in his chef's whites and she noticed how they set off the tanned skin of his face and forearms.

"Monsieur Gillou, how are you?"

"All the better for seeing you," he said, putting out a hand for hers. "I thought you might not show up for our little challenge."

This time, when he raised her hand to his lips, she wasn't surprised by his action. Only by the response it generated across the surface of her skin. She shivered momentarily.

"If you knew me at all, you would know that I always keep my word," she said, forcing half a smile so it wouldn't sound so severe.

"Hopefully, I will know you a lot better by the end of our time together," he said.

Yes, he was charming and, by God, she found him attractive. But she'd come here on a mission to make him realize the error of his ways, that the health-giving benefits of food were just as important as the taste. He'd certainly never be able to convince her otherwise. But now wasn't the moment to start an argument.

"Your restaurant is stunning," she said.

"Your first visit." It wasn't a question. This was the type of restaurant that would know if you'd been before. "You have an overnight bag?"

"Yes," she said, turning to fetch it from the back of the car.

"Leave it," he said, catching her by the arm. "I'll have someone put your car in the garage and your bag in your room."

He led her into the building through a small side door, rather than the main restaurant entrance, but she was still impressed. He led her into a small sitting room, hung with dark-hued oil paintings of wilting flowers, decaying fruit and dead game, rich and sensuous despite their gore. A wide-necked vase stood on the mantel piece, crammed with deep red blooms, and the scent of lilies hung heavily in the air.

Lisa crossed the room to look out through the small, leaded windowpanes. A redbrick terrace gave way to steps leading down to a typically French parterre—a checkerboard of small, immaculate flowerbeds full of thyme, lavender and rosemary. Beyond, a dark green lawn undulated down a slope toward a perfectly circular lake with a fountain at the center. Her breath caught in her throat. She'd heard that Le Petit Pois and its environs were beautiful, but this was perfection on a grand scale.

"A feast for the eyes," said Laurent, coming to stand next to her at the window. "Can I offer you a coffee?"

So this how the seduction would start. With something as simple as a cup of coffee.

"Please," said Lisa.

Smoky and fresh, if the small black coffee she enjoyed a few minutes later was an indication of things to come, her taste buds would indeed be seduced.

"You asked me here for two days," she said, looking Laurent squarely in the face. "Wouldn't one meal serve your purposes?"

Laurent's eyebrows rose.

"No. One dish will serve my purpose. But it will take us two days to prepare it."

It was Lisa's turn to raise her eyebrows.

"Us?"

"*Oui*. You will assist me today in the preparation. Tomorrow, we will eat it together. Then you will understand."

"Understand what?"

"That the pleasure one mouthful can afford you is as valuable as all nutrients this dish will be bursting with."

"A healthy dish from your kitchen? I hardly believe that. Tell me what it is."

"In honor of your name, Lisa—a summer pudding."

Could she have heard right?

"A summer pudding? But that's so … British … and so simple."

"And so perfect for my culinary seduction."

Laurent's smile made Lisa's stomach somersault. She tried to hide the flush of her cheeks behind the tiny coffee cup, but she wasn't even fooling herself.

The kitchen of Le Petit Pois was positively futuristic. A stainless steel pod, hidden deep within the Tudor paradise, manned by a crew of white-uniformed, young men and women. Lisa noticed most of them sported the same tattoo on their left bicep. A row of peas, nestled in a gaping pod.

Lisa was given a set of chef's whites to change into. No one had asked her for a size, but they fitted perfectly and her name had been embroidered on the chest, in the exact spot where Laurent had the three gold stars on his. Even so, she felt self-conscious walking into the kitchen.

Laurent's acolytes ignored her as she went across to where Laurent was waiting beside a stainless steel work surface. The kitchen was completely silent, apart from the sounds of knife against board or fat sizzling in a pan. Everyone appeared to know exactly what they were supposed to be doing—they got on with the work with no drama. It was utterly unlike the professional kitchens Lisa had seen on television, in which the chefs swore at each other and threw pans around.

"We start by preparing the dough for the brioche."

"Brioche for the summer pudding? That's unusual. Most recipes call for stale white bread," said

Lisa.

"Most recipes …" was all Laurent said. His tone said the rest.

They worked quickly, Lisa silently following instructions, fascinated to watch a master chef at work. Laurent told her small details about the ingredients as they went along.

"This butter, we churn it ourselves."

"I import the flour I use for breads and brioches from a small mill in Picardie."

"These eggs are laid by our own speckledy hens."

They mixed a smooth golden dough in a large steel bowl, Laurent gently schooling Lisa on her technique with the wooden spoon.

"Now the most important part. We must knead the dough to relax the gluten. Just briefly."

Laurent sprinkled flour onto the surface of the worktop.

"Give me your hands."

She held them out and Laurent clasped them with his, then frowned.

"Come."

He hadn't let go of her hands so she had no choice but to go with him. He led her through a thick steel doorway and the air around them was suddenly cold. Sides of meat hung in rows from hooks on the ceiling—they were in the cold store. Without warning, Laurent stopped, opened a stainless steel lid in the shelf in front of him and plunged both hers and his hands into a vat of ice cubes.

"Ouch!"

Lisa tried to pull her hands out but he held them in place with an iron grip.

"The brioche dough is one of the richest, the heaviest in butter. If you try to knead it with warm hands, it will split."

"But this hurts."

"A little pain before pleasure. Your hands will soon be in the dough."

As soon as he released them, Lisa pulled her hands from the ice and shook them, dripping, in the cold air. She moaned. All of her knuckle joints experienced a dull ache, while her skin felt as if it had been burnt. She made to rub her hands dry on her white tunic.

"No! You'll warm them again."

Laurent rushed her back to the bench where they'd left the dough. He quickly flipped it out of the bowl onto the floured surface.

"Now."

He stood behind her, so close that she could feel his warm breath on the back of her neck.

"Rub your hands with flour."

Lisa took a small handful from the flour bag that stood open on one side of the bench. She rubbed her hands together to coat them. Laurent reached around her on either side and did the same with his. He sprinkled more flour over the surface of the dough.

"Make the dough into a ball." His chin tickled her ear.

She tried to concentrate on his words, rather than his proximity. She scooped the dough toward her and began shaping it gently into a ball. He placed his hands over hers, making her even more aware of his body pressed against her back.

"We need to work fast. First, punch the dough."

He showed her how to use the heel of her hand to push the dough forward into the hard surface. Then how to fold it over on itself and stretch it again in a slow, rhythmic movement. As their hands moved against one another, the cold dissipated and Lisa's skin felt gradually warmer. Laurent's breathing deepened with the effort he was putting into the kneading. His body pushed against hers with the same rhythm, until Lisa became gradually mesmerized. It was almost like dancing. It was almost like fucking. She watched his fingers working on the dough, barely aware that her breathing now matched his own. As she pushed forward on the dough herself, she couldn't help but push back against him. Against the hard evidence of his arousal in the small of her back.

"How do we know when we've done enough?" Laurent spoke quietly, but his voice sounded loud in the quiet kitchen.

Lisa glanced around—the other chefs were taking no notice of them. Laurent's cheek burned against her own like a hot kiss.

"Tell me," she said.

"Feel the dough. Has it changed since we started?"

Lisa stopped kneading and pressed the ball gently with her fingertips.

"It's springy. Not so sticky."

"That's enough. Now we leave it to prove for a few hours."

Laurent stepped away from her and Lisa felt as she'd shed a warm coat. The back of her body felt exposed. She sighed, watching as the owner of Le Petit Pois placed the ball of dough onto a metal tray and covered it with a damp cloth.

"This is a proving drawer where it can rise," he said, pulling open a steel cabinet and placing the dough inside. "We'll come back later to bake the brioche."

Lisa leant back against the worktop, brushing a flurry of flour off the front of her tunic.

"You have good hands," said Laurent. "Excellent technique."

"Thank you," said Lisa, looking down at her hands as color rose again to her cheeks. She'd spent many hours of her childhood kneading dough and baking bread with her beloved grandmother—a formidable home cook who'd awakened Lisa's own interest in food and nutrition.

"I must oversee the lunch service now, Lisa. Change out of your whites and go to the small sitting room. There will be sandwiches there for you. I'll come back as soon as service is over."

In the privacy of her luxurious bedroom, Lisa stripped off the chefs whites and tossed them onto a chair. She stood in front of the full length mirror, contemplating what she saw. A young woman with a dusting of flour in her hair. Her chest rising and falling unnaturally fast when she thought about the pressure she'd felt in the small of her back. Her hand went to the front of her briefs. There was simply no denying it. Laurent Gillou turned her on.

And it was something she couldn't afford to indulge if she was to win this challenge.

She pulled on dark jeans and a white cotton top, then went quickly downstairs to her solitary lunch. Smoked salmon sandwiches on soft rye bread, along with a small glass of champagne. Regardless of whether she won this damn challenge or not, she might as well enjoy the pleasures of Le Petit Pois. It was certainly way beyond her budget to come here as a paying guest and, as the reviews all said, it was a stunning setting.

As the lunch guests left, Lisa and Laurent drove out of the front drive of Le Petit Pois in a Land Rover which, to Lisa's mind, had certainly seen better days. Laurent had reappeared moments earlier, now dressed in tight jeans and a dark red polo shirt. He gestured for Lisa to follow him and the sight of his denim clad rear climbing into the car had Lisa chewing on her bottom lip all the way down the drive.

"Where are we going?" she asked, as Laurent accelerated onto the main road.

"To the farm."

That Le Petit Pois had its own farm should have come as no surprise at all. After all, she'd already seen the care Laurent took over the selection of his ingredients.

"For the berries?"

"Of course."

Berries. As far as the eye could see. Lines of strawberries, rows of raspberries, stands of currant bushes with red, black and white berries glistening between the leaves. Blueberries in troughs. Loganberries. Gooseberries. Tayberries. Cherries in an orchard. Golden raspberries and white strawberries.

"What's a boysenberry?" Lisa had thought she knew all of the berries.

"It's a cross between a raspberry, a blackberry, a dewberry and a loganberry. Open …"

Laurent deposited a black-hued berry on her tongue. Lisa closed her mouth and crushed it against her palate, letting the sharp juices flood her mouth. She wrinkled her nose.

"A little sour."

"But you disapprove of sugar."

"Dewberries?"

"A small American blackberry. Come this way, we have some …"

They walked on between tall rows of raspberry canes. Laurent picked fruit sporadically, placing the chosen berries reverentially into the basket over Lisa's arm. They had currants and strawberries, raspberries, blackberries and a variety of their offspring so far. Dewberries followed.

"We need a few cherries," said Laurent, glancing up at the sky.

Lisa followed his gaze. Grey clouds were rolling in over the horizon.

"Cherries are hardly traditional for summer pudding," she said.

"Neither is brioche," said Laurent. "But it doesn't mean the pudding won't benefit.

The cherry orchard was at the far end of the raspberry field, where the trees had been planted on a rocky slope.

"Dark Hudson or pale Rainier?" Laurent held up two types of cherry.

"Dark Hudson for the color ..."

"But Rainier for the taste. We'll have some of both."

They picked for a few minutes in companionable silence until Lisa felt a cold drop of water explode on her arm. Then another and another.

"Oh hell!" she said. The last thing they wanted was for the berries to get wet—it would dilute all the flavors.

Without saying anything, Laurent peeled off his polo shirt and quickly wrapped it over the basket of berries. He took it from Lisa, sheltering it further with his body. They both peered up the storm clouds above their heads.

"The berries will be soaked before we get back to the farm," said Lisa. "What can we do?"

Whatever Laurent said was drowned out by a clap of thunder so close that Lisa felt it reverberating in her chest. She blinked. Laurent was running, away from her, away from the farm, down the slope to the far end of the cherry orchard. Without asking him where they were going, she followed, skidding on the stony ground in his wake, nearly tumbling down the hillside.

As she reached the bottom of the orchard, Lisa

saw the destination Laurent was making for. There was a stream, beside which stood a small folly in the form of Grecian temple. White columns topped with a green dome, the dark shadow of a doorway. They would be able to shelter till the rain passed.

Laurent was already inside by the time she caught up. She peered into the dark interior. Laurent had put the basket on a stone bench and was draping his wet polo shirt over a statue of a faun. Lisa stepped inside, taking a deep breath of the fusty air. The edges of the floor were obscured by drifts of dead leaves and dark water stains had created clouds on the decaying plaster of the walls.

"What is this place?"

Laurent looked up at her.

"The Temple of Pan, god of the woods. We have several of these follies around the estate. The perfect place for a lovers' tryst."

"Or to shelter from the rain."

Laurent laughed. "Of course. Are you very wet?"

There could be two answers to that question.

"I'm fine," said Lisa. But when she glanced down, she realized her white shirt was clinging to her skin. The fine lace pattern of her bra was completely visible. Self-consciously she folded her arms across her chest.

Laurent, on the other hand, seemed completely oblivious to the fact that he was standing in front of her, bare-chested. Her treacherous eyes roamed where they wanted, meandering across sculpted planes of his chest and stomach. Laurent was panting from the exertion of the run and so was she. The air that had been cold and fetid at their arrival was becoming warm and vaporous. The rain drummed relentlessly on the metal dome above their heads, a sharp tattoo that drowned out the sound of their breathing.

"We can wait it out here," said Laurent. "It'll blow over in a minute."

Part of Lisa hoped it would. Part of her hoped it wouldn't. Beyond the chill on the surface of her skin, she was acutely aware of blossoming heat. Arousal. She was in a confined space with a half-dressed man and, to her horror, she was becoming increasingly attracted to him.

"Try?" Laurent was holding out a strawberry, a luscious specimen that was slightly over-ripe.

The scent of it invaded her nostrils and without a second thought she dipped her head to take it directly from his fingers with her mouth. Laurent held it steady by the leaves as her teeth sank through the yielding flesh. She straightened up, savoring the taste, wiping the juices from her chin with her palm.

"Oh God, the flavor's so much more intense

than supermarket strawberries," she said.

"Of course," said Laurent. "The strawberries you buy are grown in polytunnels, on nothing but water. No taste. Ours take the goodness from the soil and ripen in the sun."

"Another."

"It's the same with our cherries," said Laurent, dipping a hand into the basket. "First the dark."

He fed her a ruby red orb which glinted in the poor light. Lisa bit into the fruit. It was crisp and sharp, its distinctive flavor flooding her mouth. She spat the stone into her hand and threw it out of the door.

"Now the lighter Rainier."

It tasted of cherries and nectarines and peaches all at once.

Lisa sighed. "I could get drunk on these."

She peered through the doorway. The rain was easing. They could probably leave the shelter and start back. But she had a question for her host that demanded an answer.

"Tell me, Laurent—these berries are perfect, delicious just as they are—so why make them into a pudding?"

In the small stone room, Laurent's laughter echoed sharply.

"You can ask me that tomorrow, Lisa. After you've tasted it."

His eyes held hers for a fraction too long. Heat flared.

"Lisa ..." He paused as if at a loss for words. "I want to ..."

Lisa swallowed. "What, Laurent?"

"May I?"

He stepped toward her and slowly raised his arms. She wondered what he was going to do. Then it became apparent. With infinite care, he untwined the hair elastic that secured her hair in its ponytail. When it was loose, he ran his fingers through it, arranging it casually around her shoulders.

"I'm sorry. But I've wanted to do that since we met at the studio. You have beautiful hair. It's a crime to tie it up."

"I ..." It was Lisa's turn to be speechless. He was standing so close to her now that she could smell his skin, with its overlay of cologne. Gazing into his searching green eyes, she lifted a tentative hand to his chest. "Laurent ..."

His skin was warm enough to make her suddenly shiver.

"Lisa."

Her fingers were stained red with berry juice. He took her hand and lifted it to his mouth, sucking in first her index finger, then her middle finger. When he let them go the stain remained.

He wrapped his arms around her, looking down at her.

"I want to kiss you." It was hardly a whisper, just carried from his mouth on a breath. "Very badly."

Lisa's mouth went dry but her lips parted. Without thinking, she pressed herself against his body. Warmth flooded through her as she raised her face to his.

He kissed her for what seemed like an eternity, his tongue roaming within her mouth, as his proximity overwhelmed her senses. She could no longer hear the beating of the rain on the metal dome. She couldn't smell the soft fruit—only the more elemental smell of him. With her eyes closed, she lost all sense of the space they were in, only aware of the circle of his arms.

"You taste like strawberries and cherries," he said, when he finally raised his mouth from hers.

Lisa looked over her shoulder.

"It's stopped raining. I think we can go," she said.

Laurent let go of her abruptly.

"Yes, of course. I'm so sorry."

Lisa shook her head, but no words formed in her mouth. How could she tell him how much his kiss had just turned her on? Laurent pulled on his polo shirt in awkward silence. Lisa knew she should look away but she couldn't. The pulse at the base of her throat was hammering and she wondered if there was any way of setting the memory of this moment in stone.

"Come on."

Laurent picked up the basket and guided her out into the sunshine with a hand on the small of her back. His touch burned through her shirt like a brand.

Out of her wet clothes and in her chef's whites, Lisa felt a little calmer. What had come over her? Over both of them? She felt sure that kissing her hadn't been Laurent's intention when they took shelter from the downpour. It couldn't happen again. She was here to educate the man, not let him seduce her. That wasn't part of the deal at all.

She spent several minutes brushing her hair, putting it back up into high ponytail, suitable for working in the kitchen. But as she twisted the elastic around her hair, all she could think of was how it had felt when he'd undone it. And the heavy cascade of hair on her shoulders with his fingers running through it.

"Get a grip of yourself," she hissed at her reflection in the mirror. Laurent was waiting for her in the kitchen and she needed to be the cynical nutrition expert, not a giddy girl with a molten middle.

Laurent looked as crisp and professional as ever, back in his whites. He was issuing instructions to his team when Lisa arrived, and he gave her a quick nod of recognition before resuming. Lisa was happy to wait. It was a fascinating scene. As a nutritionist, her interest in food also ran to preparation, so to see a professional kitchen in full operation was a rare treat.

Eventually Laurent appeared satisfied that he had everything under control. He beckoned Lisa to where he was standing by one of the fierce professional gas ranges.

"Taste this." He dipped a teaspoon into a giant copper pan that was bubbling ferociously on the hob. "Careful. It's very hot."

Lisa took the spoon of orange liquid from him and blew across the surface gently. Then she gingerly dipped the tip of her tongue into it. Her mouth exploded with a burst of intensity—it was the sea, captured in one tiny mouthful. Salty, briny, fishy ... shellfish, lobsters, prawns, cuttlefish, white fish ... peppery and sharp, but rich and deep. So nuanced she couldn't begin to describe it.

"Unbelievable!"

Laurent smiled. "Those are the parts of the fish and shellfish that most people throw away." He took the teaspoon back from her and tossed it into a sink. One of his acolytes hurriedly picked it up and took it to a dishwasher.

"Now, our brioche awaits."

The dough had quite literally doubled in size while they'd been gathering the berries. Laurent tipped it off its tray onto the floured surface of the work top, instructing Lisa on how to give it a final kneading. Luckily, this time he didn't feel the need to work with her, as it needed only the minimal touch.

"You'll never persuade me that this dish can be any way healthy," said Lisa, as she watched him easing the dough into a rectangular loaf tin.

"Healthy? What's healthy? Eating something bare and undercooked that leaves you unsatisfied. Or taking pleasure in a dish so delicious that it can lift your mood and boost your endorphins?"

"While boosting your cholesterol at the same time?"

"Bah! To eat healthy food would be to live a life so bland that I wouldn't be interested in extending it."

"You're talking about two extremes. I advocate a healthy balance."

"I think we must agree to disagree, *mademoiselle*, until you taste your pudding tomorrow."

After brushing the surface of the brioche dough with egg, he put it in the oven.

"Now for the fruit."

They stood opposite each other across the work bench, picking over, hulling and stoning the various berries in dedicated silence. When Laurent offered her an enormous tayberry, Lisa was pleased with herself that she had the wherewithal to take it from him with her hand rather than her mouth. Did she see disappointment flicker in his eyes? Or was that her own wishful thinking?

When the berries were all prepared, Laurent tipped them into a deep pan and set it on the stove. Lisa then watched in horror as he spooned sugar into them.

"Whoa! Stop!"

Laurent looked up from what he was doing with a roguish smile.

"I knew I wouldn't get through this step without a fight," he said.

"How much are you putting in?" said Lisa. "You haven't even weighed it."

"I've tasted the berries. I know from experience," he said with a shrug of one shoulder.

He carried on, spooning more and more of what Lisa thought of as white poison into the fruit.

"You can't really expect me to eat that," she said.

"I can, I do, and you will," said Laurent. "It's part of the deal you agreed to."

"Sugar is poison."

Laurent sighed. "It's just sugar."

"Possibly more dangerous than cocaine and

certainly more addictive than heroin."

The jury was out on these claims but Lisa wasn't above using them for effect. And she said them loudly enough to bring all work in the kitchen to a halt. The silent, shaven acolytes stared at her, mouths open and eyes wide.

"Oh!" said Laurent, his mouth round with horror. "For that, I'm putting in an extra spoonful."

Lisa couldn't bare it. She stepped forward and grabbed his arm. The spoon flew into the air. Sugar sprayed across the kitchen. The previously paralyzed cooks sprang into action, checking their works in progress for unwanted sugar, scurrying after the spoon as it skittered away and rushing for a mop.

Lisa looked at Laurent, waiting for an explosion of Gallic temper which didn't materialize. He simply stared at her, as he slowly stirred the fruit in the pan.

"I apologize," she said eventually. "Perhaps I should leave."

"I would be very sorry indeed if that were to happen," said Laurent. "Perhaps we could forget your little outburst and continue with the pudding. The brioche is done and the fruit is ready."

Lisa's brows knitted together angrily, but with regards to the challenge she felt on safer ground. Even if she had to force herself to have spoonful of the sweet concoction Laurent was creating, she knew full well she would hate it. Other than fresh fruit, she never ate anything sweet.

"Tell me what to do," she said, rearranging her face into a smile. She'd better try and get through the rest of this ridiculous challenge with all the good grace she could muster if she wasn't going to end up looking like a fool.

"Take the brioche from the oven," said Laurent, handing her a pair of silicone oven gloves.

The rush of hot air that emerged as she opened the oven door practically knocked her over. The sweet vanilla scent of eggs, flour and butter, transformed into a beautiful golden dome, was intoxicating. Lisa drew in deep, deep breaths as she carried the tin to their work area.

"Do you know how to tell when bread is properly cooked?"

"No."

"Tip it out from the tin onto the rack and then rap it on the bottom with your knuckles."

Lisa took off the gloves and did just that. The sound it made was hollow and deep, the crust crisp and flaxen.

"Perfect. When it sounds like that, it's done."

Once the bread had cooled, Laurent sliced it finely, setting Lisa to work cutting the crust from each slice.

"Just the crust, mind you," he said. "Don't waste any of the bread."

They lined a round glass dish with the slices of brioche and then Laurent fetched the pan of fruit. He tasted the juice with a teaspoon, nodding his head.

"Ha! Just the right amount of sugar."

He offered the spoon to Lisa but she shook her head.

"You'll taste it tomorrow and I guarantee you'll find it delicious," he said.

Lisa bit back her retort.

She watched as he lifted the heavy pan to pour the berries into the brioche-lined bowl. They rushed out amid a river of juice so dark purple it was almost black. But Lisa's eyes weren't on the tumble of strawberries, raspberries, cherries and currants. She was studying the corded sinews of Laurent's forearms as he slowly angled the pan, and the grasp of his tanned knuckles on its handle. Those fingers that just a few short hours earlier had run through her hair. Those hands that she had watched kneading the dough, and then imagined kneading her flesh.

The berries settled into their plush, golden bed and the indigo juice flooded the soft bread. The sharp scent of the warm fruit wafted around them and Lisa's mouth started to water.

"Now," said Laurent, putting down the pan.

"Put on the lid."

Lisa raised her eyebrows.

"The rest of the brioche."

As Lisa used the remaining slices to create a lid, tearing the warm bread to fit the round bowl, she was overcome with a desperate urge to pop a piece in her mouth. But bread was something she avoided whenever possible. Especially a sweet, white bread like brioche. Laurent watched her in silent amusement.

"Your final task for today is to weigh it down."

They covered the surface with plastic wrap, then a plate that fit the top of the bowl exactly. Laurent produced a couple of old-fashioned brass weights from a kitchen scale and placed them on the plate.

"There. Now the juice will soak through the bread to make the most beautiful pudding ever."

Then she was dismissed. Laurent was a busy man with a restaurant to run. She could amuse herself for the evening, in the grounds or in her room, and he would see her tomorrow for lunch.

Lisa breathed a sigh of relief, as she went upstairs to change out of her chef's whites. The man was so intense … No, it wasn't that so much. It was her response to him that felt intense. He infuriated her and intrigued her at the same time, and if she wasn't careful, she'd burn her fingers.

The breeze rustled the leaves like a soft sigh, calming Lisa's anxious heartbeat as she explored the moonlit garden. She'd dined alone in the small sitting room—on simple but delicious food—but she'd felt too restless to simply go to bed. Service was still in full swing in the restaurant and, as she'd walked across the darkened terrace, she'd been able to see into the bright dining room. It was spare and elegant, it's Tudor origins still discernible but toned down. The table linens and settings were all plain white. It was evident that the star was the food. Though she was too far away to see what people were eating, she could see their expressions changing, lightening, each time they put a forkful into their mouths.

Every table was taken up by couples or groups of smartly dressed diners. Most of them were middle-aged or older, but there were families with younger members, too. However, there were no children. She remembered reading on the website that children were only allowed to come at lunchtime. Through the open window, the buzz of conversation and the tinkle of glass and silverware made a distant chorus, while the swift, precise movements of the waiting staff became a stylized dance between the diners.

She saw Laurent emerge from the kitchen and watched as he made his way round the tables. Without realizing what she was doing, she moved closer to the window, to see him better. He smiled and laughed, exchanging a few words with each of his guests, most of whom were completely in awe of him. Lisa took another step closer, then realized to her horror that a woman sitting near the window was pointing at her. She'd been spotted.

She turned away into the darkness and hurried down the steps to the parterre. God, she hoped the woman wouldn't mention to any of the staff—or to Laurent—that she'd seen someone peering through the window. Her feet crunched on the gravel path, making her slow down dramatically, and she quickly took advantage of an archway cut into the hedge along one side.

She found herself at the start of a long avenue of towering chestnuts. The sounds of the restaurant had faded away, and now the soft rustling in the branches above her was all she could hear. She walked silently on a manicured grass path into which the silver moonlight carved the dark shadows of the trees. She allowed herself time to simply breathe, waiting for her heartbeat to return to normal as cool air washed over her like a balm.

In her mind's eye, she was still watching

Laurent—in the restaurant, in the kitchen, in the cherry orchard, holding out fruit to her on juice-stained fingers. Standing in front of her, torso bared, in the temple of Pan. Pulling the hair band from her ponytail and spreading her hair around her shoulders. She tugged out the ponytail she'd been wearing since her afternoon session in the kitchen, liberating heavy waves of copper, letting drifts of it fall across her face as she shook it out. She could almost taste the cherries he'd fed her, the scent of the wet fruit rising to her nostrils even now.

She walked as if dreaming until she ran out of avenue. In front of her stood another small folly, but this time with columns and a pointed roof rather than a dome. Cold air embraced her as she stepped inside and dried leaves crackled under her feet. There was no statue in this temple—just a bare, flat altar stone that took up most of the space inside. She leaned against it, breathing deeply.

She lay on her back on the cold, flat stone, imagining she was waiting for someone to come to her. Waiting for Laurent to come to her. She closed her eyes and took a deep breath. It tasted like the air in an old church or crypt. A familiar smell, but otherworldly at the same time. She shivered, wrapping her arms around her chest to stay warm.

She already knew she was wet. She didn't need

to put her fingers between her legs to find out. She put them there to make herself wetter. Easing them slowly into her briefs, her jeans only half undone, just enough to give her the space she needed. She placed her other hand on her shirt, feeling the hardness of her nipple against her palm. Her breathing quickened.

She wondered what might have happened in the temple of Pan if they hadn't stopped at a kiss. She remembered the taste of Laurent's mouth, then imagined it kissing her elsewhere. Her hips pressed down against the hard stone, urging her to explore deeper. She undid her jeans fully and slipped them down as far as her knees, then quickly unbuttoned her shirt. With knees bent and splayed, her fingers could reach deeper.

With her other hand, she slid her bra cups aside, allowing the cold air to draw her nipples to attention. The skin surrounding them puckered. She rolled one between finger and thumb, pinching hard enough to cause a sharp intake of breath. Her clit mirrored their swelling when she touched it. She kneaded the soft flesh above it with the heel of her hand, as if she was again working the brioche dough.

Laurent's hands were practiced at kneading, his long elegant fingers strong and dexterous. She'd felt his touch so briefly, but it had been enough to make her lie here on the stone alter imagining it in more intimate places. Pushing her fingers deeper still and twisting her nipple more sharply, Lisa came. Two short gasps and a long exhalation marked her climax, her knees jerking together. Her breath softened as she rode down the other side, her hand gripping the front of her pubis, waiting for the pulses to stop, for equanimity to be restored.

A twig snapped outside and Lisa's blood froze in her veins.

She sat up on the altar and hurriedly fastened her shirt as she peered out into the darkness. Everything seemed still apart from the slight sway of the branches. She held her breath and listened to the silence until her ears rang. It must have been an animal. No one would be wandering around in this remote part of the garden at this hour. It was after eleven o'clock.

She pulled up her jeans as she dropped off the altar onto the floor. She was a little shaky on her legs— she'd hardly recovered from her orgasm and the noise outside had thrown her into full fight-or-flight mode. But she knew she needed to get back to the house. At some point the doors would be locked for the night and she didn't want to have to wake some poor member of staff, or worse yet, Laurent, to let her in.

She hurried back up the avenue of trees and emerged onto the gravel path of the parterre. Ahead of her, climbing the steps to the terrace, she saw a figure dressed in white. At the crunch of her footfall, he turned to look back.

It was Laurent.

When morning came she was still trying to convince herself he hadn't seen her. The snapping twig had been an animal. Laurent had merely been taking a breath of fresh air in the parterre after a long night in a hot kitchen. But she hadn't been able to sleep, despite the luxurious softness of her bed, with its goose down pillows and Egyptian cotton sheets. What if he'd seen her, lying on that alter with her jeans around her knees and her breasts exposed? Kneading her own flesh, gasping with pleasure.

Thinking about it made her light-headed.

She looked in the bathroom mirror, expecting to see traces of her shame written across her face. But she looked the same as ever. She spent time putting her hair up into a neat bun. She would be all business today. She'd taste the pudding, give her verdict. Then she'd leave.

Breakfast was brought to her in her room, so thankfully she didn't see anyone. Specifically, she didn't see Laurent, which was the main thing. After she'd eaten—just a selection of fresh fruit and some green tea—she got out her laptop and worked on an article she needed to finish. The benefits of eating seeds. Safe territory. She would have liked a stroll in the garden but, no. Too much risk of bumping into Laurent. And she knew that if she went outside she'd be drawn back to the scene of the crime.

There was a knock on the door. Lisa glanced at her watch and saw it was just before one.

"Come in," she called.

It was one of the waiters.

"Monsieur Gillou is ready for you now in the private dining room."

Lisa took a last glance in the mirror, smoothing her white silk blouse and tucking it into the neat black cigarette pants she wore. She didn't know what she was expected to wear, but as far as she was concerned, she was working. This outfit emphasized her trim figure—a result of eating the healthiest of diets rather than the sort of cuisine championed by her host.

She followed the man down the wide oak staircase and along a corridor she hadn't been down before. There was an open door at the end. The waiter stopped, indicating with his hand to usher Lisa through. The room she found herself in was not so much small, but intimate. There was a long table, laid up with settings for two. A thick-pile carpet muted her footsteps as she walked in. The walls and upholstery were all deep red—the room seemed to wrap itself around her as the door shut behind her. And once again, a display of deep ruby lilies perfumed the air with their heavy, fecund scent.

There was no sign of Laurent, so she went across to look out of the room's small, angular bay window. Its deep alcove was fitted with a cushioned love seat—a long, low bench upholstered in plump maroon velvet. She sat down and looked out over the parterre. Beyond it, over the hedge, she could see the top of the temple she'd discovered the previous evening. She quickly looked away, her cheeks coloring. That was the last thing she needed to have seen.

The door opened and Laurent came in, looking good enough to eat. He was dressed as simply as she was—black shirt, black trousers—but the perfect fit left nothing to her imagination. As usual, there was not a hair out of place. He was followed by the waiter, who carried a bottle of champagne and an ice bucket.

"*Bonjour*, Lisa. Did you sleep well?"

Was that a loaded question? No. She wasn't going to let it be.

"Very well, thank you. And you?"

"Always when I'm here," he said, indicating to the waiter to open the champagne. "I take a turn around the garden when I finish work to clear my head, then I sleep."

Lisa wondered if he slept alone. She knew he wasn't married, but that was all she knew of his personal life. And immediately regretted starting to think about his sleeping habits.

"Champagne?"

"No, thank you."

Laurent's eyebrows shot up but he didn't say anything.

"This is a professional challenge, *Monsieur* Gillou. I don't drink while I'm working."

"I was hoping that you'd find it pleasurable, *Madamoiselle* Summers."

The sudden formality was accompanied by a *froideur* between them that hadn't existed before.

"That's not why I'm here."

Laurent smiled but there was no warmth. It made his features seem momentarily wolfish.

"I'm confident you'll enjoy our splendid pudding. But first, a simple main course."

The waiter took his cue and vanished.

Lisa looked out of the window again, turning her back on Gillou. She didn't hear him moving—the carpet deadened every footfall—but she became aware of him standing just behind her shoulder.

"My intention here," he said, so close to her ear, "is to enhance the pleasures of all of the senses. Not just taste. So, you see, my garden is a feast for the eyes and the nose, as well as providing produce for the restaurant."

"And for the ears?"

"We hold opera evenings throughout the year. Intimate concerts, by invitation only."

"They sound wonderful."

"See beyond that hedge?" He stepped forward to stand next to her and pointed. "My little temple of Aphrodite. It makes the perfect backdrop for a romantic aria."

Lisa turned away sharply. So he'd seen her. She felt sure of it now. This whole encounter was becoming increasingly awkward. She went towards the table to sit down, only to find herself exasperated when Laurent beat her to it, gallantly pulling out one of the chairs for her. The table was long and narrow, the other place setting was at the opposite end. At least it would put distance between them.

The waiter returned, followed into the room by two underlings, each bearing a silver-domed tray. With huge theatricality, the first waiter lifted each dome in turn to serve them their food.

"Steamed dover sole with raw asparagus," said Laurent, as his staff left the room.

"This is very healthy," said Lisa.

"I'm sure it is," he replied, with a vague wave of his hand. "I took it from an article you wrote. It's not something I would serve in my restaurant but I didn't want to take any of the attention from the *pièce de résistance* to come."

Lisa ate in silence. The fish, though beautifully cooked, had virtually no flavor. The asparagus was hard and crunchy. Certainly in no way a pleasurable experience compared to the food she'd eaten here so far.

"Asparagus is a power house of vitamins," she said. "Keeping it raw preserves them."

"It makes me very sad to eat food like this," said Laurent.

They continued to eat in silence and neither of them finished their food. Laurent stood up and pressed on an old-fashioned bell button next to the fireplace. A moment later the waiter appeared in the doorway, making Lisa wonder if he'd been standing just outside the room.

"The dessert, please, and a bottle of the 2003 Tokaji Essencia."

"*Oui, monsieur.*"

He cleared their plates.

"Thank you, Paul," said Laurent.

Lisa's heart pounded in her chest and her hand shook as she raised her water glass to her mouth. She looked up at Laurent to find him staring at her intently.

"So, Lisa, that was your kind of meal. It seemed

a very frigid affair. If that was all the pleasure my life afforded me, I'm not sure I'd want to prolong it."

"Eating isn't the only pleasure, Laurent." It was time to fight back. "Good health is a pleasure you don't appreciate until it's gone. And then it can be too late."

"Your way offers no intensity, no sensation."

"And yours too much. You can surely admit that overindulgence dulls any of your sensory pleasures."

"For you, there would be no danger of that happening."

Why did his words sting so much? Was she really so buttoned up that she couldn't enjoy a few simple pleasures anymore? What about the previous evening? She'd abandoned herself to the sensual when she was alone, in the temple of Aphrodite. She watched him watching her. And it dawned on her that she'd been caught in a very clever trap. If she allowed her senses to be seduced by Laurent's creation, he'd be proved right. He'd win and she'd lose. But if she resolutely held out against the sensuous in favor of the purely healthy, what would it tell the world about her? He would still be the winner. She would be the frigid loser.

Did she want to lose on her terms or his?

The door opened and Paul reappeared with his team. One of them placed a huge silver dome in the center of the table, while the other set down a crystal jug of cream, and then proceeded to show Laurent the bottle of Tokaji.

"Would you like me to open it, *monsieur*?"

"Leave it," said Laurent.

They trooped out in single file, Paul last, closing the door slowly and deliberately behind him.

The moment was upon her. She made up her mind.

"I'd very much like to try that wine, Laurent. I understand that Tokaji is something special."

"This Tokaji," said Laurent, picking up the bottle as if it were made of something even more fragile than glass, "this Tokaji is exceptional. One of the most sought after wines in the world. To make Tokaji, the vintners wait until the grapes are rotten. The intensity of the flavor …"

Words seemed to fail him. Lisa watched in silence as he slowly withdrew the cork from the bottle until it came free with a resounding pop.

"This wine is from 2003 but a good Tokaji can be kept for up to two hundred years."

He poured a small amount into two of the dessert wine glasses already on the table.

"Taste it."

Lisa picked up one of the glasses and took a small sip. She let the thick, syrupy liquid flood her tongue and was rewarded by an explosion of honeyed sweetness that carried a bitter twist of burnt apricot in the tail. For a moment she forgot to breath. As she swallowed she became aware of a further complexity, flavors blossoming on her palate that she simply had no names for.

Still standing beside her chair, Laurent took a sip from his own glass. He watched her as closely as ever, but his eyes widened as he, too, succumbed to the flavor of the wine.

"It's like … nectar," said Lisa. It wasn't but she didn't have a better word.

"That's what they call it." He took Lisa's glass from her hand. "Now, for our pudding."

He returned to his own end of the table and unceremoniously dragged his chair back towards Lisa, leaving a gullied trail in the heavy carpet.

"You're too far away from me. We should enjoy this together."

While Laurent lifted the silver-domed platter to what was now their end of the table, Lisa fetched the remains of his place setting. She positioned them in front of his chair, which was now at ninety degree angle to her own at the corner of the table.

"Will it be a blind tasting?" she asked.

Laurent burst out laughing. "Certainly not," he said. "Before you even taste it, I want you to devour it with your eyes. How food looks is as important as how it tastes." He caught hold of the looped handle of the dome. "When you take a lover, Lisa, you appreciate him as much with your eyes as with your sense of smell, taste and touch, don't you?"

"Of course." A blush rose to her cheeks.

He lifted the dome and Lisa gasped. The pudding had been turned out of its bowl and sat, glistening like a giant cabochon ruby in center of a silver platter. The intensity of red, the sumptuous surface of the juice-soaked brioche, the tart smell of the fruit that she could taste at the back of her mouth … When her hands gripped the edge of the table, the pudding quivered as if it were alive. Bright juices bled from it onto the silver like blood from a beating heart.

"It's beautiful," she said, barely a whisper.

"Ah, but wait until you see the inside," said Laurent softly.

He picked up a silver cake slice and plunged it into the center of the pudding. He breached the outer layer of brioche, then Lisa heard the serrated blade rasp as it plowed through the berries within. A quiet click as the tip of the slice touched the plate beneath. Laurent extracted the cake slice and made another cut, separating a wedge from the whole. Deep dark red, ruby, scarlet, crimson, black, white and purple, the berries tumbled out in a wash of magenta juice. Lisa's mouth flooded with saliva. She heard Laurent's sharp intake breath.

Seizing a deep-bowled serving spoon, Laurent lifted the slice of pudding onto one of the plain white dessert plates, piling it high with excess berries and drizzling it with a flood of juice. He reached for the crystal jug and, with a flick of his wrist, a dollop of thick white cream ran in an avalanche down the outer slope of brioche.

He put the plate down in front of Lisa.

"*Voila! C'est magnifique, n'est-ce pa?*"

Lisa understood but she was speechless.

Laurent dropped into his chair, angling it away from the table to face Lisa. He took the white linen napkin which lay crumpled beside her place setting and held it up to her.

"Allow me?"

"Yes ... of course."

With deft fingers, he secured the napkin around her neck.

"It's so juicy ..." he said, by way of explanation.

Lisa didn't care. She fervently wanted to taste the pudding. She was literally panting for it in a way that she'd never experienced before. She picked up her spoon but Laurent put his hand over hers. His touch was warm and firm. A sly shiver slipped up the back of Lisa's neck.

"Not so fast, *chérie*," he said.

Lisa raised her eyes to his face.

"Look at it first, drink in the colors, taste the scent of the berries. Imagine the textures of your first mouthful."

His thumb rubbed the back of her hand and goose bumps blossomed up her arms. Her breath caught in the back of her throat. Her mouth, watering a moment ago, now seemed dry.

"Please ..."

She didn't miss the momentary flash of triumph in Laurent's green eyes as he took the spoon from her fingers and dug it into the purple mound between them. He raised it to her lips with a single, blood red strawberry on it.

"The strawberry gives the base note of the flavor," he said. "And look, it's a cupid's bow, the pout of a young girl who's never been kissed."

She opened her mouth as he let it slip from the bowl of the spoon. It landed on her tongue and she immediately tasted the familiar flavor. But there was so much more—a hint of raspberry, the sharpness of the currants blunted by the sweetness of sugar, a wave of vanilla from the brioche. She crushed it against her palate with her tongue and, as she breathed in and out, the scent of summer was overpowering.

"Now these beautiful loganberries," said Laurent, raising the spoon again to her mouth. "They lift the taste with a cut as sharp as a razor blade across your tongue. Without sugar, you'd bleed."

It was true. They carried an acidic kick that sliced through the sweet juice, making Lisa's breath hiss.

"Something sweeter to make up for it." Raspberries. "The top note of the bouquet, standing to attention like bare nipples in a cool breeze."

Their eyes met as Lisa slowly drew the berries into her mouth. Dark hair drifted across Laurent's forehead. As she bit into the raspberries, Laurent's other hand tugged off the napkin from her neck. He dropped it and then his fingers brushed, quite deliberately, against one of her breasts. He held her gaze and Lisa felt her nipple pebbling beneath his touch. She swallowed and took a deep breath.

"More …" Her voice sounded as thick and heavy as the cream.

Laurent took his hand from her breast and she looked down to see a crimson fingerprint on the white silk. Behind it, the dark purple shadow of her nipple showed through. Laurent's breathing quickened, but he turned his attention back to the pudding. He used the spoon to cut through the bread, scooping up a juice-soaked strip of it, smeared with a white crest of cream.

"The best part," he said, feeding it to her. "As soft, as delectable, as the flesh between your thighs,

Lisa."

The cool, velvety brioche melted in her mouth, buttery and elastic, its sweetness infused with the flavors of the berries, tempered by the luxurious curve of cream against her tongue. She savored the texture and clung to the taste. She didn't want to swallow. She wanted to keep it in her mouth for ever. One perfect mouthful of joy.

Laurent got up from his chair with quiet deliberation.

"Excuse me," he said. "I have to do this."

He went around to the back of her chair and stood behind her. She felt the pins that held her bun in place being slowly withdrawn. She heard the sigh as they were dropped to the floor. As she finally swallowed, she felt her hair cascading around her shoulders. Laurent's hands ran through it, sweeping it to one side as he bent to kiss the nape of her neck.

He slipped one hand into the front of her blouse, cupping her breast. Lisa sighed. Heat flooded between her legs and she bent her neck as his lips traversed it.

"I knew as soon as I saw you in Dexter Dixon's studio that I had to make this pudding for you."

He leaned forward over her shoulder and reached for the spoon. A cherry stranded in a ruby pool. As Lisa took the piece of fruit, Laurent's hand trembled. Juice ran down her chin and dripped onto the front of her blouse, spreading like bloodstains through the fine weave of the silk.

"A cherry nestled between the folds of brioche." He took a deep breath. His meaning was quite clear to her and, high up inside, her muscles clenched against nothing. "I need to taste you, Lisa," he whispered.

She hardly knew what she was eating now. Spoonful after spoonful, ever more seductive in flavor and texture. White currents, like tiny pearls of pre-cum, red currents that burst sharply on her tongue like a lover's bite, strawberry kisses, silken swirls of cream, rich and satisfying …

"Do you surrender?"

"I surrender."

"Again."

"I surrender."

He was mesmerized.

"I surrender."

As she uttered the words for the third time, Laurent swept the pudding, the plates, the glasses, the jug of cream, the bottle of Tokaji, silver candlesticks, all of it to the floor with the arc of his arm. There was a tremendous crash. He pulled Lisa up from her chair, kicking it away behind her. Juice and wine soaked into the carpet at their feet.

"I need you. Now."

Lisa's leg hardly had the strength to stand. She

had to put a hand on his shoulder for support.

"You want me, too." It wasn't a question.

"Yes."

Laurent pushed her back so she was leaning against the edge of the table. He ripped her blouse open and dragged it off her shoulders as she kicked of her shoes and undid her trousers. Ten seconds later she was lying naked on the gleaming mahogany. She felt a rogue berry bursting under her shoulder as she shifted her position.

"*Mon dieu*, I …" He didn't get any further than that. His hands were at the hem of his shirt to pull it off but he didn't manage to.

He sprawled full length along her body, his mouth finding hers, then moving to each breast in turn, kissing her neck, biting her shoulder until she winced with pain. His hands explored her torso, tracing the outlines of her ribs, delving into her navel, caressing her stomach, skimming the soft mound that rose at the apex of her thighs. He pushed her arms above her head roughly so he could first breathe deeply of and then kiss her armpits.

He slipped off the table, sliding her along it until she was in the perfect position for him to bend his head low and taste her. He pushed her legs apart, dipping his tongue between them. Lisa started, smacking her heels on the hard table, but Laurent held her hips steady. His tongue roamed into and across the darkest, most intimate spaces of her body.

He paused for a second and raised his head.

"Stay," he murmured.

Lisa wasn't going anywhere.

Laurent dropped an arm over the side of the table. When he raised it back up Lisa caught a glimpse of berries and cream. A shock of cold on her labia caused her to gasp, then Laurent's tongue was back, licking the mingled juices that ran freely from her pussy. She arched her back and pushed her hips forwards against his face, relishing the scraping of his stubble on her soft flesh. She could still taste the berries in her mouth, feel the texture of the spongy brioche on her tongue and, as she climaxed, she raised her head to see Laurent's face, purple stained, smiling as he looked up to watch her come.

He slid along her body, not caring how much juice he got on his clothes, and Lisa lay back, slipping down the far side of her orgasm with the satisfaction of feeling his weight pressing against her. As he came within reach, she clawed at his shirt, desperate for her own taste of his flesh, needing to feel the heat of his skin against her own.

Temporarily sated by his first taste of her, he paused long enough to let her tug his shirt over his head, dropping it over the edge of the table into the fruity morass beneath.

Lisa could see a damp stain of pre-cum on the front of his trousers. Her mouth watered. She quickly undid them, dragging them down his thighs. Free of constraint, his cock surged and hardened.

"Let me taste you now," said Lisa.

Laurent climbed off the table, letting his trousers and shorts fall to the floor.

"Here," he said, gesturing. He moved to the far end of the table, beckoning her to follow. Still on her back, she slid up the flat surface until she was able to hang her head over the edge where he stood. Reaching up with her hand, she was able to guide Laurent's cock into her mouth. He tasted as salty as the pudding had been sweet, equally delicious. She lapped at him with her tongue and then he took over. He placed his hands at either side of her head and she relaxed into the cradle they formed. He started to fuck her and she let him thrust deeper and deeper towards the back of her throat. The table beneath her creaked and shuddered as they moved in unison.

"My God ... I want to come ... But I need to fuck you."

He stopped abruptly, withdrawing from her mouth, leaving a salty trail of pre-cum in his wake. Lisa savored the taste as he gently moved her back down the table and fetched a cushion from the window seat to put behind her head.

"Yes, fuck me, Laurent," she whispered, as he climbed back up onto the table.

She spread her legs and he opened the path between her lips with eager fingers. His cock slid into her and a frisson of expectation took flight from her belly to settle at the back of her throat. He drew out and sank back in. Each time he did, the sensations which spiraled through her body intensified. He teased her nipple with his teeth and she hooked her legs up behind his back.

"Laurent ..."

He pressed a hand down between their roiling hips. Fingers circled her clit. He kissed her. She bit his bottom lip, hard. It made him fuck her deeper, pinch her harder. She cried out and he stifled her noise with his tongue against hers.

Finally they soared, mouths grafted, bodies entwined, bursting like ripe fruit with juices and sweat mingling on their skin.

At one.

Exhausted.

Smiling.

"What will you say to Dexter Dixon about your

triumph?" she said a little later, slumped back against his chest, still naked. They were comfortable now, resting on the soft upholstery of the window seat. Her body and his were stained pink and indigo with fruit juice, smeared with sweat and semen and her juices, sticky with spilled wine.

"Bah!" exclaimed Laurent. "Dexter Dixon is a fool. I'll tell him nothing."

"You're not going to go back on his show with the story of my seduction?"

"It's none of his business."

Lisa closed her eyes.

Later still, Laurent Gillou offered Lisa Summer a job as nutritional consultant to Le Petit Pois.

Many kisses later, Lisa Summer said yes.

Summer Pudding Recipe

A sweet and juicy summertime treat!

2lbs 3oz (1kg) mixed berries – raspberries, strawberries, currants in the main

4oz (100g) sugar, plus extra to taste

14oz (400g) brioche loaf (or similar sweet white bread), sliced

1lb (450g) bag of frozen mixed berries

Double/heavy cream to serve

1 glass bowl, 4 pints (2 liters) capacity

(These quantities do not need to be hugely accurate—and particularly the amount of sugar required depends on how tart the berries are and your own taste)

1. Put the 1kg of fresh berries into a pan with 100g of sugar on a low heat, stirring occasionally, until the sugar has dissolved and the berries are releasing their juice. Continue cooking until the berries are soft, but still holding their form. Taste the juice and add more sugar if required.
2. Cut the crusts off the brioche, losing as little of the white bread as possible.
3. Line the bowl with plastic wrap/cling film.
4. Line the bowl with the slices of brioche, reserving approximately 1/3 of the slices for the lid.
5. Spoon the warm fruit into the brioche-lined bowl.
6. Use the remaining slices of brioche to create a lid.
7. Cover the lid first with a layer of plastic wrap/cling film, then a flat plate as close as possible in size.
8. Weigh the plate down with heavy objects (e.g. tin cans).
9. Refrigerate overnight.
10. A few of hours before serving, put the frozen berries into a pan and cook down vigorously until the berries disintegrate.
11. Push the berries and their juice through a sieve to make smooth, rich, juice. Leave it to cool.
12. Take the pudding out and remove the weights. Spoon the cooled juice onto any white patches of bread on the lid. If there are still patches of white bread showing at the sides, use a table knife to gently prize the pudding from the side of the bowl and spoon some juice into the space. Reapply the plastic wrap/cling film, plate and weights until ready to serve.
13. To serve, remove the plastic wrap/cling film, plate and weights & turn the pudding carefully out onto a plate. If any bread still looks pale, pour a little juice over it. Serve with the remainder of the juice and a plenty of fresh cream.

THE LOVE APPLE

ZAK JANE KEIR

The Love Apple

Names have power, he knew that. His only previous girlfriend, Amanda, had a tendency to talk about the subject from time to time: the cultural significance of names and how many names a person might have and who could use them. She'd once talked to him about the meaning of names: hers meant "love" or "beloved" and his, Lee, meant "a clearing", though apparently a lot of kids called Lee had been named after a US General on the side of the slave owners— at least that was how she'd put it to him. She'd been quick enough to say she didn't think there were any intimations of racism or even revolutionary tendencies in him despite his name. Lee, as quite often happened when Amanda was off on one, had just smiled and shrugged and passed her another packet of cashew nuts.

She'd been into all these odds and ends of information: she had a degree in anthropology but worked in a bookshop, which was how he'd met her. Lee loved books, but fiction was what did it for him, rather than the various philosophical or theoretical or self-help books Amanda was so fascinated by. Sometimes she would talk about writing a book herself, but as far as he knew, she never actually made a beginning.

Very close to the end of that relationship, there had been another discussion about names, but this time it had been about nicknames and pet names. She had noticed, she said, that the two of them didn't have any kind of special names for one another.

"You don't like being called Mandy, though. You've always said that," Lee had protested, and she'd clutched at her hair in rather exaggerated exasperation and said, "That's not what I mean, you're not listening." He'd apologized at once, reluctant to have an argument. It had crossed his mind to kiss her and suggest that he make it up to her for his inattention by paying her some more direct, erotic attention, as they were side by side in her big, brass-framed bed at the time. Somehow, though, he already knew that it wouldn't work, and neither would cashew nuts. Amanda was going to have her say.

"Most couples call each other things like Big

Bear, or—or Babycham or something. Special names that other people don't understand. Think of all those ads they used to have in the papers on Valentine's Day, all these really peculiar nicknames that meant an awful lot to people, they were fascinating. And even normal pet names, like whether you call someone babe or darling or sweetheart, which one you choose matters, it's part of you and part of your relationship. And you and I don't even do that."

Lee had waited, silently, partly because he didn't know what to say to reassure her and partly because the whole subject of nicknames made him uncomfortable. Eventually Amanda had dropped the subject, but had opted for sleep rather than sex, as had been happening more and more frequently. It had only been a week or two later that they had decided, without much discussion, to see less of each other, and then less and less until they just weren't seeing each other at all.

Lee hadn't been as badly upset as he expected he would. He'd known, probably from the second or third date, that it wasn't going to be any kind of lifetime commitment, but at the time he'd been delighted enough that clever, pretty Amanda had been willing to spend time with him in the first place. He wasn't clever, though he wasn't stupid, either; he didn't think anyone would describe him as pretty. Good manners and a fondness for books didn't seem to be the greatest asset when it came to dating.

Now he was single again, though, he felt brave enough to take his first, tentative steps onto the fetish scene. He'd read just enough novels which depicted kinky sexualities to give him the idea that it might be something he would enjoy, but had always known that it wouldn't be something he could share with Amanda. Her tastes tended towards the gentle and sensual with vague overtones of romantic mysticism, which had been alright by Lee but somehow not quite enough. Perhaps he would find out who he really was by exploring his slow-burning fascination with whips, handcuffs, spanking and high-heeled footwear. At least, he hoped, he would have fun trying.

It was fun, exciting fun, at the beginning, even if it wasn't quite as exciting as he had dreamed it might be. The bulk of those he met were not unfriendly, but nor were they falling over themselves to make him welcome. He realized fairly quickly that unassuming, slightly plump young men with heads full of yearning dreams about the ultimate mistress were over-represented in these circles; and he might have retreated into a solitary life of fantasy if he had not been determined to at least be part of this—to him— endlessly tantalizing underground world.

After a while, he found his feet a little, made a few friends, even got as far as participating in a scene or two. He still had hopes. Though there were not very many unattached women to be found, there were plenty of people up for at least a play session within a club. The first time he bent over a padded whipping stool, his raised buttocks bared to the air, bared to anything, he thought he might come when the first spank landed on his quivering flesh. He hadn't, then, been sure if it was against the rules to lose control of yourself to that extent and had been afraid to ask. As it was, the spanking was a sharper sensation than he expected and his cock, which had been urgently throbbing against the curved, vinyl-covered top of the whipping stool, softened in surprise. It wasn't until he was back home, alone in his single bed, that he really obtained an erotic charge from the experience. He fucked his own hand, quickly and efficiently, re-imagining the scene in the club: groaning and writhing as the woman—he had forgotten her name but she was lithe and blonde and flamboyant—brought the palm of her leather-gloved hand down on his ass, again and again and again until the spunk burst out of him, a messy little explosion on the club's nice dungeon furniture. He saw the surrounding club goers laughing or expressing distaste, even pictured himself being ordered to lick his own emission from the vinyl cover.

His body seemed to burn with shame as he reached a genuine climax, rather than a fantasy one, but he fell asleep almost instantly.

He had reached what he felt was a kind of equilibrium by the time Martyn reappeared in his life. He hadn't found a regular partner, not even someone to play with on a casual basis, but he remained optimistic and was happy to have made a group of new friends. Now and again, he would encounter a dominant woman who liked to have several submissives to play with in the course of an evening, and he began to discover more about his own likes and dislikes. He wasn't particularly enthralled by elaborate rope bondage, either on him or on anyone else, but whether he preferred the slow build-up of a soft flogger or the intense, speedy sting of a cane seemed to vary depending on his mood, and the attitude of whoever was wielding the implements in question. He was also comfortable with various tones and styles: light-hearted oh-you-naughty-boy raucous roleplay, sessions that were all about sensation and skill and, very occasionally, the ones that involved more blatant sexual elements. He had never reached a climax during a club session, though from time to time he had seen others do so. Whether public orgasm and unmistakably sexual activity were acceptable seemed to vary from club to club: at one large-scale event held in a venue that usually catered to swingers, he had watched, enthralled and painfully aroused, as a stately and quite mature woman in a long skirt and corset bent a younger woman and a man over a waist-high bench, side by side, and thrashed the pair of them, using a variety of implements. When the buttocks of both naked submissives were well-warmed, their Mistress gave them some murmured instructions or advice, and the man got up onto the bench, lay down on his back and let everyone see that his cock was fully erect, the tip of it gleaming with moisture and the foreskin fully retracted. The naked girl stood beside him, with her hand between her legs, and Lee was close enough to see that she was sweating a little and quivering with unmistakable excitement. He wasn't close enough to be one of the two men the Mistress called forward to help the girl climb up onto the bench and mount her naked partner, but he had a pretty good view of the couple's ecstatic fucking. This scenario featured in his fantasies for several months afterwards, though he often recast the submissive girl as some other model or actress who had caught his eye. He sometimes liked to alter other details, such as the Mistress joining in with the fuck, and he began to contemplate the possibility of non-traditional relationship structures and opportunities for himself.

The night he ran into Martyn, he was cheerful and almost relaxed, and the last thing on his mind was the reappearance of someone who had bullied him unmercifully a decade or more ago.

It might not have been so bad had Martyn been another punter in the club. Martyn as an adult would surely have developed enough in the way of social skills to hide his own mean, patronizing character or at least to see the funny side of it rather than loading his barbs with something thermonuclear in terms of the damage done. There was also the matter of scene etiquette, which tended to disapprove of cruelty that wasn't pre-negotiated and consensual. While banter was engaged in from time to time, it was cautious unless taking place between good friends: there seemed to be an unspoken but widespread understanding that there was a degree of fragility to the shared illusion that everyone within the sexual playground was desirable or potentially so, living out his/her fantasies in a place of acceptance. Open mockery of another's appearance or failure to meet mainstream aesthetic standards of youth, beauty, fashion sense or slenderness was likely to mark you out as a tourist, a mundane, someone who didn't have any manners.

Martyn was there as a photographer, representing one of the websites dedicated to cataloging and exploring various subcultures, and Lee would later discover that the club's promoters had rapidly begun to regret allowing him to attend at all, despite their initial enthusiasm for the publicity the website might offer.

Lee hadn't recognized the other man at first. He'd been aware there was a photographer present, but had stayed away from the corner by the cloakroom where a backdrop and a couple of lights had been set up. He knew his own looks were nowhere near striking enough to be of any particular interest, though he wasn't particularly concerned that a picture of him in a fetish club would cause problems in his everyday life. Working in the payroll department of a large haulage firm didn't mean your private life had to be beyond reproach, except with regard to your personal finances. As the evening progressed, he'd become aware of annoyance among various other clubbers, and overheard a few comments to the effect that the photographer was both clueless and a "rude prick", but, again, it hadn't seemed to have any relevance to Lee himself.

It was only when he went to the bar to get a round of drinks that his and Martyn's paths had properly crossed.

The photographer was temporarily on his own, waiting to be served, and something about his profile jarred in Lee's memory. He tried not to stare too blatantly, but it only took a few seconds before he'd placed the guy. Martyn Stock had been feared by at least half the school, but not because he was the biggest or could punch the hardest. It was his unfailing talent for spotting and announcing other people's weaknesses that had made him so lethal. He'd been a scrawny runt in his late teens, with a pointed nose and chin and fair hair cut brutally, unfashionably short; and he was always badly dressed but no one had ever dared to comment. Now his hair was longer, with a slight tendency to curl, but his features were as sharp and ferrety as always. He wore black jeans with black DM boots, and a black T-shirt with the logo of another fetish club on the front: clearly this was as much effort as he was prepared to make to comply with the evening's dress code. Lee himself was wearing what was then his usual attire of PVC shorts, his silver snake bracelet and unbranded black low-heeled boots. It was a warm night anyway, and the club was crowded enough for him to have worked up a slight sweat even though he had, as usual, steered clear of the dance floor. He didn't think he'd gone particularly red in the face, but even as the thought crossed his mind, Martyn looked across at him, frowned and then grinned a joyous, shark-like grin.

"Fuckin' hell, Tomato! It's you, isn't it?"

There was probably a space of a second or so in which Lee could possibly have denied all knowledge, could have made a comment of polite indifference and walked away, but even then he knew, on a deep and despairing level, that it would be useless to do so. Martyn had never been the type you could overcome by pretending indifference or ignorance of what he was talking about. The asshole had always been far too determined to have his bit of fun. And before Lee could begin to frame the first sentence of dismissal, the familiar heat had spread across his face and down his neck and he'd blushed deeply red in the most self-betraying manner he could imagine.

It was all over for him then. He'd sometimes wonder, in subsequent months and even years, if that shouldn't have been the end of his exploration of the world of kink, right then and there.

Martyn attached himself to Lee for the rest of the evening, merrily regaling just about every one of Lee's friends or acquaintances with tales of their schooldays, most of which were exaggerated or twisted to make Lee look stupid. He had never been a genius, but had not, in his estimation, been anything like the dickhead Martyn was now portraying. And, of course, pretty much every conversation Martyn started carried the extra taint of the fucking stupid nickname they'd all found so hilarious all those years ago. Lee Rosso: red by nature, red by name, always has a face of shame! At some point, he had fleetingly remembered Amanda and her rant about "pet names"—no wonder he hadn't ever been inclined to go down that route with her.

It still might have made no difference, or been forgotten after their single encounter, but Martyn hadn't just been the photographer for the website. The bastard was writing the copy as well as putting up the pictures, and three whole paragraphs of the piece were given over to "My old schoolmate Tomato, never would have thought he'd turn out to be a pervert." Martyn hadn't gone as far as sneaking a picture of him, of course. The photographer obviously knew the limitations under which he was obliged to operate, and had not suggested that Lee pose for him, not even with his face concealed. Enough people had heard Martyn talking to and about him for word to have spread, and that was all it took.

Lee submitted, he had no choice but to do so. Names have power, Amanda had said and, with no other option, he would embrace the power of this one. Tomato at school had been the butt of every joke, Tomato the kinkster would not be. Having previously only lurked on web forums like KinkSters and avoided any adult-orientated stuff on Facebook, he signed himself up to those fetish sites that allowed a user name, calling himself Mr. Tomato. Online, he discussed books and music, and BDSM protocol, and ventured an occasional apposite joke. He never, ever whined and always stayed well out of the periodic ruckus that exploded when some male newbie started objecting to the dearth of single women on the club scene. Other people, he thought, liked him well enough but it slowly dawned on him that the persona he'd adopted was getting in the way of his own potential gratifications. He was jolly, he was friendly, he was self-deprecating, and somehow he felt less and less able to put himself forward on the infrequent occasions when a House Domme or another woman who was in the mood to play with multiple submissives made it known that she was ready for willing victims. From time to time he would attempt to make his wishes known to someone he found attractive, but found himself being politely, kindly, almost unknowingly rebuffed. Slowly, very slowly, he began to turn bitter.

He fought against it, or at least he fought against making it obvious to others. He did his best to restrict how much online time he spent in the type of forum filled with other men protesting about being friend-zoned. He wanted to retain his humanity, and hold his awareness that no woman owed him a hiding, a sexual encounter or even a conversation if she didn't want to engage with him. He didn't blame women for his situation, he blamed himself. From time to time, though, he tried too hard and the rebuff was sharper, more crushing. He barely even blamed Martyn Stock any more. He'd built himself a trap and now he was in the jaws of it, and would remain there forever.

His fantasies grew darker: no longer did he dream of beatings that shifted from pain to pleasure, but of endless frustration and embarrassment. Sometimes he was forced to serve as a footstool or even a seat, ignored and forbidden to speak while all around, other slaves had their wishes gratified in some form or other. From time to time, he imagined blundering into someone else's scene or tripping over as the whole of the room turned to laugh and deride him. He began to be scared of inadvertently offending or outraging other people, and controlled his own behavior to the point of finding every night in a club more of an endurance test than a source of pleasure.

He met the woman who would change his life on one of the nights he had decided to make a determined effort to enjoy himself. He would be polite and friendly, would avoid brooding in corners, would also steer clear of the clusters of single men who spent most of their time complaining to one another about the lack of women, even when there were lots of women on the premises. He had not been to this particular club before; it was relatively new and the reviews board on

KinkSters bore several positive comments.

The evening got off to a reasonably good start, as he ran into a couple he had gotten to know slightly in his—and their—early days on the scene, but hadn't seen for some time. Catching up with their news enabled him to relax and enjoy a relatively ordinary conversation. Even when some other acquaintances of theirs came to join them at the large corner table they had obtained, he still felt unusually comfortable. The main subject under discussion was a notoriously bad book about BDSM, on which everyone had an opinion, whether they had read it or not. Lee, who had read nearly all of the supposed BDSM classics, began to enjoy himself as the good and bad points of various fictional floggings, restraints and erotic tortures were debated. People came and went at intervals, but the only one he really noticed was the petite but imposing woman with the exquisitely elegant clothes. He thought he remembered her from the almost-swingers event at Renegades, but he couldn't be sure and didn't feel confident enough to ask. She was older than many of them, he thought, and perhaps that was why she had chosen an almost Victorian style of outfit rather than something shiny, tight and revealing. She had on a white blouse with an open, lacy collar and a dark brown leather corset, and she wore several large rings. Her hair was quite long, and she had left it loose rather than pinning it up in the sort of antique style her outfit might have suggested. Perhaps she did that because it was so striking: mostly a dark gray but with one paler streak that might or might not have been natural. She said little, but he was aware of her listening intently. Lee wondered if she had a slave or submissive with her that evening, as everything about her made it clear she was dominant. The talk turned, at some point, to erotica writers' choice of pseudonyms, a subject Lee found interesting almost despite himself, and at this point the gray-haired woman joined the discussion more directly.

"Using a pseudonym doesn't mean you're ashamed of what you write, it's more about making a statement about your work. It's only become complicated now that authors are supposed to sell themselves along with their stories. Why shouldn't you pick a glamorous, romantic name if you're writing about passion and excitement?"

Lee knew he'd never quite looked at the subject of names in quite this light, and sat back a little, turning over his thoughts so he didn't suddenly say something crass and stupid. He did his best to be discreet while he gazed at her, knowing that he wanted to know more about her.

From time to time, he noticed that she was looking in his direction, even studying him, and he actually began to consider approaching her directly. Then a big bearded man with two subbie girls on leads came over to the table, calling out greetings to the people sitting on the far side of it, which meant that everyone reshuffled to accommodate the newcomers, and by the time it was all sorted out, not only had the direction of the conversation irrevocably changed, but the woman in the corset had gone.

He spent most of the rest of the night in the manner to which he was more accustomed: wandering from the bar to the dungeon to the edges of the dance floor and back again. He tried to tell himself he was not really looking for her; that he didn't know her and there was no reason to suppose she would have any interest in interacting with him, but he kept on scanning the club, hoping for a glimpse of her pure white blouse. Surely that alone would make her easy enough to spot among the black rubber, leather and PVC that most other people were encased in. Little by little, his enjoyment of the event began to fade, and after a while he decided to head for home before he could spoil his own night any further. While he was waiting for the cloakroom, he saw her again, now with a black sheepskin coat over the white blouse. She had a silver-topped black walking cane, he noticed, and couldn't help asking himself if it did double duty across a deserving bottom from time to time. He tried not to stare in a manner that might offend her, but she noticed him anyway, and paused beside him.

"You're very well-read," she said, and then she touched his arm lightly and moved away. Even when he'd been waiting twenty minutes for the night bus, he imagined he could still feel the imprint of her long, slender fingers on his skin.

There had, about a year ago, been something of a uproar on KinkSters when someone was trying to make contact with a particular individual by posting a description and demanding to know if anyone had and could provide a phone number, likely location or "at the very least" an email address for the person concerned. Lee thought that it might not have turned quite as vicious had the original enquirer had the sense to appreciate, when reminded, that not everyone wants to be tracked down by online randoms, certainly not by those who display enough entitlement to describe an email address as "the very least" they could be given. Still, remembering the amount of venom that had splattered over the discussion made him very wary of posting even the most tentative online inquiry as to the identity of the mature, elegant dominatrix with the walking stick. He did not, after all, know her name, which would make it difficult to claim any kind of proper acquaintance with her. He contented himself with fantasizing about her, dreaming up various scenarios in which she had him in restraints of some kind or another and thrashed him soundly, or otherwise tortured him into a state of unbearable ecstasy. He alternated between searching KinkSters and other fetish-related websites for anything which might conceivably be a mention of her, and leaving his laptop switched off in favor of re-reading selections from the more literary of the erotic novels he had accumulated over the years and remembering the tone of her voice when she had praised his taste in books. He was profoundly convinced that he would see her again, but superstitiously aware that there must be steps he needed to take before it could happen.

He went to a couple of munches, he went to a couple of clubs, and there was no sign of her. He told himself, repeatedly, that there would be some kind of cosmic indication, that he was being made to wait until the time was right. Then one night she was there, and he initially wished with all his heart and soul that she hadn't been.

The club had been uncomfortable for him from the start. Though Martyn Stock had never reappeared on the fetish scene, there were enough people who had read the piece and absorbed the mean, short-sighted attitude it epitomized to make certain clubs, on certain nights, hotbeds of an unhealthy type of sex-related suffering. The reminders were almost continuous: you are not beautiful enough, wealthy enough, cool enough, your desires are contemptible. All the things you might want are on display but you can't have them and shouldn't even presume to want them. Though he had been to this club before, more than once, the atmosphere on that particular night was a toxic mixture of the arrogant and the desperate, and Lee, longing both for the mysterious gray-haired woman and for something—anything—to relieve his loneliness, found himself blundering about like the worst sort of loser. Eventually, he found himself next to a pretty girl in an exquisite silver latex catsuit, jostled against her by the crush in the corridor. She wore silver stack-heeled thigh boots and carried a short single-tailed whip, which he accidentally bumped with his arm.

"Back off," she snarled at him, but her expression was more amused than angry, or so it seemed.

"You could punish me for bumping into you, if you like," he blurted. He cursed himself for saying it as soon as the words were out, and would have apologized, but she turned away with a disgusted sigh and said, not to Lee but to the nearest other people, "This place is just crawling with short, fat wanky men, isn't it?"

He backed away, scrambled away, pushing

through the crowd, face burning with shame. Finding the door which led out to the smoking area, a small yard with a broken patio heater and a tarpaulin stretched between two walls to keep the rain off, he stumbled outside because it was easier than trying to fight his way to the main door. Unusually, the area was deserted, and Lee made his way to the high metal table in the far corner and slumped against it. After a while, hating himself and everyone else, he began to kick the central pole that held the table up. And then he began to cry.

"What's the matter?" The voice was familiar, but for a moment or two he couldn't bring himself to look up and see who was addressing him. He had a terrible feeling he knew, and she was the last person he wanted to see—or rather, to have see him in this state. He thought that if he remained still and quiet, the speaker might take the hint and leave him alone. Then he would compose himself, get his coat, go home and give it all up for good. But it occurred to him that, at any moment, someone else might come outside and catch him blubbering like an idiot, and that was enough to make him raise his head. There she was—of course it was her. Tonight she was wearing midnight blue, a long tailcoat over tight trousers tucked into boots, and her hair was in one thick plait over her shoulder.

Her face showed infinite patience as she repeated the question.

"What's the matter?"

She came right up to the table and rested her elbows on it, propped her chin on her hands and looked at him expectantly. Lee took a long, shuddery breath and told her. Not just about the incident with the girl in silver, but the whole miserable story, because there was no one else to tell and he couldn't bear to keep it to himself anymore. He told her how he knew he was giving off the wrong signals and making a fool of himself, but he didn't know how to change and felt like a failure. He told her that he wasn't a pest or a creep but was terrified he might turn into one. And he told her that he was going to go home, delete his KinkSters account and forget about the fetish scene.

"I don't think that's necessary," she said. "I think I can help. I think it's a matter of perception."

He walked back through the club, one pace behind her, matching his steps to hers. The lead she had him on was not very long, and probably not particularly strong, being only a thin strip of leather. He was very careful not to snap it. She had produced the collar first, and then the cuffs, and only when he had put them on did she bring out the lead. He did tell her that he had never worn one before and she gave him a brief outline of how she expected him to behave once she had fastened to the steel ring in the front of the collar. He had been worried that he might be clumsy and trip over or bump into her or something, but people tended to get out of her way without her even needing to ask. Some of them looked him up and down, some of them looked at her, but if anyone's gaze was hostile, he didn't notice it.

The play space was not particularly big and, at that stage of the evening, not particularly busy. A small group of people had gathered around a wooden rack to engage in some kind of sensory play with a bound and blindfolded figure that Lee couldn't see well enough to ascertain the gender of, and a giant of a balding man had a slender, red-haired woman wearing nothing but hold-up stockings tied to an A-frame in the furthest corner. He was teasing her with a spiked wheel though there were marks on her thighs and rear suggesting he had previously caned her.

Lee's current mistress, as he was beginning to think of her, led him to a set of stocks and unclipped the lead from his collar.

"It would get in the way," she observed, and tucked it back into her bag. She spent a moment or two just looking at him, assessing him, and he felt his skin prickle into goosebumps. He had heard others say, from time to time, that a gaze has weight, that you can feel when someone is looking at you, but he had never fully understood what they meant until then.

She lifted the upper bar of the stocks and ordered him to bend over and put his head and his hands in the appropriate places. When he complied, she lowered the bar and locked it in place before pulling his PVC shorts down to his knees and running the palm of her hand lightly over his bare backside. Her skin was soft, and felt slightly cool against the flesh of his ass. His cock stirred, and he tensed his muscles, not sure if he should control himself. He wasn't sure he could control himself, but he decided to try.

There was music playing in the dungeon zone, something quieter and more sedate than the usual electronica and vintage house that this club, like most others, favored for the dance floor. It was at a low enough volume to make it easy for him to hear every word she said.

"Some people call this play, and some people call it punishment," she said. "I like the term 'discipline', or even 'ritual'. You can think it over and decide for yourself, later. For now, let's say it's a way of removing your wrong ideas."

The first implement she used was a flogger with a great many tails of soft, thick suede. He had seen similar ones on stalls at the fetish markets, but not often in use. The impact of this one seemed at first to be far too light, but he intended to trust her. Raising objections would do nothing but put an end to the experience, and that was the last thing he wanted to do. She used it mainly on his bottom, but from time to time laid it across his shoulders, sometimes lashing him lightly there, sometimes trailing the ends of it down the length of his body. After a while, a slow, almost dreamy warmth began to spread through him, and when his prick unfurled and stiffened, he no longer felt the need to worry about it. The impact of the flogger changed, and he realized that this was because she had replaced the first one with another. He guessed it was made of leather as it stung a little more, but the growing intensity of the blows was still sensual rather than challenging.

She paused, at some stage, and ran the palm of her hand over his buttocks, squeezing gently, rubbing and almost—but not quite—allowing her fingers to stray down the crack of his ass, and he moaned.

"That's good," she said. "Good. Pleasure is good, but pain has its uses."

She stepped back, as far as he could tell, and there was a long, still, silent moment when he felt intense anticipation tinged with alarm. Though painful whippings had featured in his fantasies, he had never experienced more than a short-lived sting or two from a paddle, or very occasionally a cane. He wondered what she might be about to do, and whether or not it would be bearable.

It was a paddle, rather than a cane, he realized, when she laid on the next few strokes. He couldn't tell what type of paddle without turning his head, and he hadn't been given permission to turn his head, so he stayed exactly where he was as smack after smack fell harshly on his buttocks. The flogging had already heated his flesh, and at first the blows she administered simply increased his excitement. After a while, though, he began to find them harder to take. He gasped, and then he let out a couple of expletives, and the beating stopped. Nothing happened, then. Nothing at all. He wondered if he should move, or speak, or remain in position. His bottom didn't actually hurt as much as burn with a steady kind of heat. He felt slightly dizzy and his mouth had dried.

A hand ruffled his hair. It was her hand. Then he was aware of her bending over him to whisper in his ear.

"I could push you further," she said. "I could make you scream. Your ass is as red as a tomato, but right now it feels good, doesn't it?"

He realized, after a pause that was possibly a bit too long, that she expected him to answer, and he did.

"I don't know how I feel. I think I like it."

"An ass as red as a tomato," she repeated, and then pulled his shorts up, smoothing them over his tenderized skin. Next, she raised the piece of wood that had held him in position, and told him, in a louder voice, to stand up and look at her. Her eyes were clear and bright and there was something like affection on her face.

"Well done," she said, and put her arms around him, holding him close and stroking his back, stroking his hair and cupping each of his buttocks with a gentle squeeze and a tender pat or two.

His cock was still hard, but the urge to come was somehow simply not there. He felt far too relaxed to want to touch himself, and the idea of asking her to touch him any more intimately than she was doing right now didn't even occur.

"Let's go and get a drink," she said, finally taking a step or two backwards. Lee nodded, dumbly—he didn't think he was capable of speech just yet. He had a momentary flash of anxiety when they reached the bar, as he only had a certain amount of money on him and the drinks weren't cheap. However, she produced a twenty, handed it to him and instructed him to order two single malts. He did as he was told—no other option was imaginable and once he had procured the drinks and handed back her change, she refastened the lead to his collar and took him, lead in one hand, plastic tumbler in the other, to the end of the bar. She sat on a stool and grinned at him with an air of ageless mischief.

"It is quite customary for a gentleman to stand in the presence of a lady, and I think at present you will find it more comfortable anyway," she said, and raised the glass.

"To good times and better."

They didn't leave the club together, but they did both leave shortly after finishing their drinks. It was fine with Lee, he had her name—Elinore—and her KinkSters handle, which was XElinoreX. They spent much of the following week in private online chat, and she invited him over to her place on the Sunday afternoon. They would, she said, make further explorations, and Lee didn't try to press for any more information. Their discussions had been a mixture of teasing hints, puzzles and challenges that had excited him far more than any outright declarations of taking him as her sub or what she might expect from him would have done. For his part, he'd just done his best not to come across as an idiot and he felt that he'd acquitted himself reasonably well. Surely he must have done, to have received the invitation in the first place.

When she opened the door she was wearing scarlet PVC: a waistcoat with nothing underneath it and a pencil skirt with a zip up the front. He saw the scarlet seams on her sheer black stockings—he'd spotted the tell-tale tiny bumps in her skirt—as she walked up the hallway ahead of him. She hadn't given him any instructions about how to dress himself, so he was in plain but smart black trousers and a simple light gray shirt.

He had time to notice that the flat was mostly light and airy, a white-painted, wooden-floored main room and hallway, and then she had led him into the bedroom, which was all done in blacks and dark reds—a lavish, decadent boudoir with a shelf of implements and toys next to the bed.

"Strip," she said. "This is your next lesson."

Once he had complied, she made him lie on the bed, and cuffed his hands to the top rail and his feet to the bottom one. There were no quilts or pillows in evidence, just a black silk sheet that was cool and slippery against his skin. The curtains were closed, and when she shut the door as well, the room was lit only by the lamp on the bedside table. There was no sound apart from his breathing, and hers, for several minutes. He thought he might hold the picture in his mind forever: Elinore quite still, quite close to him in the warm, gloomy room, in her scarlet PVC; a little calm, considering smile on her face.

"Think about this," she said. "Does the Dominant exist for the pleasure of the submissive, or is the pleasure of the Dominant the reason for the submissive's existence? Is it both, or neither?"

She took a black leather blindfold from a drawer, and fastened it over his eyes. Then there was another of those silent pauses that lasted for a time he couldn't calculate the length of. It didn't matter; he didn't mind. The messages they had exchanged had brought him to a point where he trusted her entirely and felt no fear. He was ready for her, ready for whatever she might be going to do.

She used her fingertips at first, nothing but her fingertips. She trailed them over every inch of his body, and every nerve ending seemed to spring to life under her touch as she explored him. Up and down and side to side, finding the spots that tickled and the spots that made him shiver and all the places where his flesh responded, she stroked and teased and caressed. After a while, she began to use her nails, scratching lightly then more fiercely, and he heard himself begin to moan and pant, felt himself harden and began to tense his buttocks and, unable to help it, thrust his pelvic area upwards. He heard her giggle, but it was a fond, encouraging giggle rather than one of derision.

A long-nailed finger traced a circle round the puckered rosebud of his asshole and a line between his anus and his balls, and then he felt a hot, moist dabbing at the head of his prick.

    Oh fucking hell, it was her tongue. She was licking his cock. She was licking the head of his cock. Lee cried out in amazement and her lips enclosed him. She began to suck, and he writhed and jerked in the cuffs, his fists clenching and unclenching, his toes curling, his breath coming in snorts and gasps. She sucked him harder, clamping his rod between her tongue and the roof of her mouth then releasing the pressure, only to slide her lips down close to the root and back up to the tip, and doing it again and again, and he wondered in a frantic flash of thought how he'd managed not to lose control already, and how on earth he was going to stop himself coming any minute. From his chivalrous soul he called out a warning, "I'm going to— I can't— Oh god I'm going to—" and those fingertips tickled his balls and those soft strong lips, rather than pulling away, sucked harder and he gave up completely, let himself go, and the bursting, spurting, joyous ecstasy of his climax made showers of stars seem to flare against the inside of his eyelids.

    A short time later: he couldn't tell how long, he felt the mattress yield and then the cool, slightly sticky texture of her PVC clothing against his naked skin. She touched his shoulder, then his cheek, and then she gripped his chin and kissed him. He could taste a little saltiness on her lips which must have come from him but she didn't, as he had half expected, feed him his own spunk back from her mouth.

They lay together quietly, and then he felt her shift away.

"I'm going to take the blindfold off you now," she said. "And then the cuffs."

Once these things were done, she got off the bed and stood, smiling down at him. Lee's limbs felt too heavy to move, but he didn't feel inclined to sleep. He blinked and glanced towards the window, but the curtains blocked out whatever light might remain outside. He realized he had no idea what time it was, or how long he had been in her company.

She seemed to catch his thoughts without him speaking them aloud.

"It's about quarter past six," she said with a lingering grin. "There's a shower through the door to the right of the bed. Dress again afterwards and come through to the front room."

She was sitting on a long, low, pale green sofa when he made his way into the room he'd only glimpsed on arrival. It was, much as his original impression had been, light, clean, uncluttered and soothing, and he could smell something faintly spicy and tempting coming from the kitchen area at the far end.

There was a coffee table in front of her, but instead of coffee it held an open bottle of wine and two filled glasses along with a steel pot of cutlery and a stack of napkins.

"Come and have a drink," she said. She had taken off her high-heeled shoes and lifted her stockinged feet onto the sofa, something Lee found somehow endearing. However, she swung them down onto the floor, making room for him, and patted the space beside her, making it clear that he was to sit rather than kneel. This was not the sort of Mistress-slave protocol he had sometimes read about, but he found he didn't care in the least.

"How do you feel?" The question wasn't asked abruptly, but he jumped a little, all the same.

"Good," he said. It sounded inadequate, so he tried to elaborate. "Really good. Thank you. I, um, thank you. But I didn't, you know, you didn't get …"

"It's fine. That wasn't the idea."

She sipped some wine, and he, almost unconsciously, imitated her. It was a warm red and he thought it tasted expensive.

"You had started to think of yourself as undesirable, and you were wrong."

She put her glass down and got to her feet.

"The food should be just about ready. No, stay where you are."

He stayed. He was never going to disobey her, even though he was aware that it was fairly uncommon for the Mistress to be the one cooking and dishing up the dinner.

She returned with two steaming bowls of spaghetti and sauce, which she set down on the table before re-seating herself, and Lee saw that the mixture was a rich, orangey red. It did smell delicious and, despite his nickname he had never gained a distaste for the sauce.

"Tomatoes," said Elinore, as he bit his lip and looked at the floor. "Have you any idea how special they are?"

He shook his head, and she took a fork, plunged it into the mixture, expertly twirled up a mouthful and neatly devoured it. He was unable to resist doing the same, and let out a little moan of appreciation at the first taste of the rich, salty succulence.

"They call this Spaghetti alla Puttanesca— Whore's Spaghetti," she went on. "It might sound like a silly name, but it doesn't stop it tasting good."

She ate some more.

"It isn't even that silly a name. Do you know what the old name is for a tomato?"

Lee, just about to swallow, couldn't answer but decided no answer was required.

"A Love Apple. People used to consider them aphrodisiacs. Dangerous aphrodisiacs that would imperil young men and women's immortal souls by inflaming them with carnal passions. They're red, they're juicy, they're sensual."

She began to eat again, with lascivious enjoyment. Lee watched her tongue dart around her lips between each forkful. He ate as well, savoring the food and the wine, a sense of great wellbeing spreading through his body.

"Later," she said, "You can show me just how much of this is true. I believe, my young tomato, that you owe me at least one orgasm."

I owe you much, much more than that, Lee thought, but an orgasm would be a good place to start.

A Dance of Ocean Magic

Elizabeth Black

A Dance of Ocean Magic

The tang of citrus invigorated Sierra Palmer as she sliced into a blood orange. Her blood rushed through her veins, and her skin tingled with excitement. She stood in her kitchen, cutting up fruit for a salad she had dreamt of making for nearly two months. Her exhilaration colored everything in her view, giving her beach house a magical aura. She looked at her expansive living room and patio and smiled at her good fortune. Her home nestled on the northeastern Massachusetts coast amid salt marshes and ocean breezes. She had inherited it from her mother and her grandmother before her. All three women practiced ocean magic, and the location so close to the roiling Atlantic only strengthened their powers. Sierra closed her eyes and prayed to the ocean goddesses Yemaya, Lady Asherah of the Sea, Amphitrite, and Cymopoleia, wishing for the warm touch of the man of her dreams who would appear at her doorstep very soon.

The reflection of the setting sun on the window glass gleamed pink and gold; a beautiful tableau that warmed her heart. The glow reflected off her ocean blue walls. Her cat walked across the floor, stretched, and headed to his bed for a nap. That creature didn't have a care in the world, and Sierra envied it. The crisp smell of salt water wafted about her, and she inhaled to take in the briny scent. Waves crashed on the beach. Seagulls called in the distance amid the roaring surf, setting a mood of romance and enchantment. She felt gloriously alive, and her evening was only beginning. The French doors to her patio stood open to the unseasonably warm weather. The day felt more like a lazy spring than the end of winter. A storm brewed far out at sea—a Nor'easter but she refused to allow the threat of a squall to ruin her evening. She shivered with excitement over the thought of Tibor Dali knocking at her front door any moment now.

She tossed blood orange slices into a casserole dish and stirred with two large wooden spoons. Exotic fruits filled her salad—sumptuous treasures like blood oranges, dragon fruit chunks, and lychees. She tossed in some maraschino cherries since Tibor mentioned how much he liked them. She mixed the fruit with coconut, sour cream, and a little honey—a recipe handed down to her by her mother, but with her own decadent twist. Her mother used pineapple chunks, grapes, mandarin oranges, and pear slices. Sierra wanted to feed Tibor unusual seasonal fruits that were neither canned nor available every month of the year. The blood oranges in particular were in season only in March. She had a narrow window to work with, and she wanted her salad to have that extra special allure.

The sight of Tibor Dali made her go weak in the knees. His enigmatic nature hinted at the more famous Dali, Salvador, but they were not related. The artist was Spanish while Tibor was Hungarian. His surname meant imposing and virile, and Tibor's demeanor reveled in both. When she first spied him thumping a cantaloupe in the produce section, his ruggedly handsome face set her heart racing. He smoldered like a fire god, his intense gaze falling upon her as if he could see her naked body beneath her sweater dress. She blushed and turned her head away, but before she could catch her breath she saw his two-toned Italian leather shoes in her line of vision.

He pulled off a day's stubble looking like he just rolled out of bed, and she doubted he was alone. Whoever he was, his manner screamed old world— tweed trousers, sweater vest, silk tie and linen shirt beneath a camelhair coat. A white silk scarf around his neck made him look like he belonged in another era. If she hadn't known better, she'd have though he just walked out of an F. Scott Fitzgerald novel.

It took two months of small talk for her to get up the nerve to ask him to join her at her home for fruit salad and a bottle of bubbly. His preferred drink was champagne, and he promised to bring a bottle as well as some of his native Hungarian dishes. She joked and asked him what he was celebrating. He replied in his delicious accent that every day he enjoyed life gave him a reason to celebrate, champagne or not. That accent teased her with promises of an exciting evening sipping Moët and slipping into an embrace so thrilling her head would spin. She couldn't let that opportunity pass by without taking advantage of it so, two weeks ago, she'd asked him to join her in her home.

She picked up a small blue glass vial from the windowsill over her sink. *No, not that one.* She didn't want to cast a love spell with those drops. It was too powerful. She wanted Tibor to fall for her on his own, without too much help from her magic. She only wanted to use her magic to nudge him along in her direction. A practicing witch who learned her craft from her healer mother, Sierra ran her fingers over her collection of tinctures. The bottles nestled on her windowsill amid purple mussel shells, bleached sand dollars, and slipper shells she had gathered from the beach. All were useful to her own brand of ocean magic. She picked up a clear glass vial containing purple liquid, poured a teaspoon into her salad and stirred well. Her spell ensured she and Tibor would enjoy an evening of easy relaxation with a hint of lust that neither of them would ever forget.

Would he like her offering of food in exchange for his attentions? She chose the ripest and freshest lychees that she peeled and pitted herself. The taste of the delectable little round white fruits reminded her of Moët and Chandon, a fitting treat for so exotic a man. As she stirred her salad, bits of white dragon fruit with their small, dark spotted seeds caught her eye. The pear-like taste of dragon fruit mixed well with the champagne quality of the lychees. The purple liquid she poured from her vial of magic gave the salad a touch of peppermint. Would her gift impress Tibor? Did she really want to impress him? Why not simply enjoy his company?

Sierra lacked the confidence to believe she could attract Tibor of her own accord, so she allowed her magic to do the heavy lifting. Amber resin incense burned on her living room coffee table in the center of an amethyst crystal she set aside specifically for this occasion, its warm scent promising hours of romance. She dipped six taper candles in rose oil and set them out on her dining room table, blowing on each wick until the flame sparked to life. Rose oil encouraged love and lust, and she craved both. She had read her tarot earlier but the message of the cards had been confusing and elusive. Sierra was never very good at predicting her own future.

She inspected herself in the large mirror overlooking her couch. How did she look? At 35 years of age, she had settled comfortably into her body. Her chestnut brown hair behaved itself for a change. It fell in waves to her waist. Despite the approaching storm, it did not frizz. The royal blue cotton sweater and skirt couldn't prevent her from shivering, although she was not cold. In her nervousness, she hoped Tibor would admire her outfit as she knew she would be swept away by his elegant choice of clothing. Although he appeared to be in his late 40s, he seemed ageless. The man pulled off his classic look with elegance. She stood sideways and inspected her small frame. She did not consider herself to be especially glamorous, but overall she liked her shape. She was neither too fat nor too thin. She was just right.

At five p.m. sharp, there was a knock at her door. Her heart jumped to her throat. What would she say? Would she stumble as she greeted him? Would she say something bone-headed and cringe at her own words? She swallowed hard, walked to the door, and opened it.

Tibor stood before her, or, rather, a bouquet of red and pink roses poked their blushing faces at her as Tibor peeked from behind them with a wicked grin on his handsome face. He had trimmed his stubble without shaving it off, a look that made Sierra's mouth water. On any other man it would look like unkempt five o'clock shadow. Tibor made it look rugged and wild. His blue-gray eyes flashed the color of the churning Atlantic, reflecting the urgency she felt in her breast. He held a bottle of champagne and a cloth bag in his other hand. She wondered if he was as anxious as she was over their first intimate meeting, but he didn't seem to have a nervous bone in his body. Tibor was always at ease. His affable nature relaxed Sierra's quaking resolve, and she felt the tension leave her body a little at a time.

"Good evening, Sierra. You look lovely. That shade of blue becomes you," he said. So Tibor did notice her outfit. Why should she expect anything different? His attentiveness attracted her as much as his virile good looks. She stood aside to allow him into her home. "You live in a beautiful location."

"That's the reason I chose to live in this beach house. My mother left it to me in her will after she died five years ago. You can't beat the view. I can go to the beach any time I wish." She took the flowers, and headed for her kitchen to find a vase.

"How old is the house? It looks like something out of a mystery novel."

"It does have that Daphne du Maurier look, doesn't it? It was built in 1930, as a beach house for doctors who lived further inland. My grandfather was a surgeon." She smiled at him and breathed deeply, wishing away a flush that warmed her cheeks. "Thank you for the roses. They're beautiful. I love roses. I rarely get them."

"I wanted to give you a special gift for our first meeting. We've spent so much time chatting over oranges and raspberries that we've never met outside the fruit aisle. It's a pleasure to be with you. The dinner is still warm, but you might want to heat it up in the oven for a little while."

He smelled of dreams and promises amid cedar and cinnamon, making her heart race. His fingers brushed hers as she grabbed the bag, and his touch sent electric sparks up her arm. Before she could dwell too much on her nervousness, she took the bag from him and pulled out two foil-wrapped baking dishes. They were warm to the touch, but they didn't burn her fingers.

Thunder sounded in the distance. Tibor's presence seemed to encourage the turbulent ocean. She practiced magic and made the most of her gifts, especially this evening, but Tibor possessed an earthy magic of his own. Her heart danced and her breath caught in her throat at his mere presence.

She turned her oven to 200° and placed the dishes inside. Moving quickly, so as to fully enjoy his company without any distractions, she grabbed a vase, filled it with water, and placed the roses inside. She set the vase on the kitchen counter, admiring how the blush from the roses enhanced the purple crackle glaze of the vessel.

Once she took his camelhair coat and hung it in her closet, she invited him to sit on her couch alongside her. Clannad played in the background, but the gentle Celtic music didn't drive the electricity from the air. Skin tingling with excitement, she sat as stiff as a soldier waiting for a bomb to drop. Legs pressed together and hands clenched in her lap, she allowed a little distance between the two of them. Tibor, ever the gentleman, kept to his side of the couch. He held up the bottle.

"A little champagne? I hope you like Moët." His serene attitude reflected in his languid pose. He looked much more relaxed than she felt. He also looked so delicious she fought hard to keep from touching him. He wore a cream-colored jacket over a pale pink cotton shirt with an ascot at his neck. Not many men could pull off an ascot. Tibor seemed to have been born wearing one. His double-breasted waistcoat enhanced his broad chest and flat stomach. Light tan trousers covered strong and well-formed legs. He even wore wingtips. The man was as European as could be, which was only fitting as he hailed from Budapest.

The loud pop of the cork made her jump. His mellow voice lulled her into a romantic mood as he poured bubbly into two glasses. "I brought a dish my mother used to make for me, and I've mastered it. Paprikás Csirke."

"I don't know what that is."

He smiled. "Yes, you do. It's chicken paprikash. I'm sure you'll like it. Do you like paprika and sour cream?"

"Yes, very much."

"It has both. It's hot, spicy and meaty."

Just like you. She resisted adding that little commentary. "You're right, I have heard of it. I'm looking forward to tasting it."

"It's usually accompanied by dumplings, so I brought along some nokedli."

"Those are dumplings?"

"Yes. They're small, like rice. Very filling, too." He handed her a glass. "I would like to propose a toast." He held his glass high. "To the lovely woman who introduced me to the wonders of Norwich, Massachusetts. Without her, I would be lost."

She smiled and sipped her champagne. The

crisp taste rolled over her tongue. She wanted to eat, but she didn't want to be too full, because she intended to make room for him as dessert. "I can't wait to eat your dinners. Both sound delicious. I've wanted to try your native food ever since I met you."

He placed a hand on her shoulder, a movement so casual she didn't even jump at his touch, but he lit a fire inside her as his fingers pressed against her sweater. "Now you have a chance to taste what I have to offer."

Was that an accidental double-entendre or was he tempting her? She resisted commenting how she wanted to taste him something fierce. "The food will take awhile to heat up. Would you like to try my fruit salad now? I can't wait for you to taste it."

"I'd love to. It's hard to believe we met only two months ago over the oranges and raspberries at the grocery store."

Two months, two days, and six hours ago, but she wasn't going to tell him that. How quickly should she move? Would he overtake her before she had a chance to seduce him? Did she even want to seduce him? Being a bit of an old-fashioned woman, Sierra wanted Tibor to woo her. She wanted to be swept off her feet as her heart leapt. Making small talk was only part of the seduction. "I couldn't resist talking to you. I've never met anyone like you before." She stood, and he followed suit. He also followed her into the kitchen.

"I put some unusual fruit into this salad." She said. "You can only get it certain months of the year. Here, try this." She dipped a spoon into the salad, and pulled up a small bit of fruit—a lychee. The smell of coconut and mint from her elixir floated in the air. He smiled as he inhaled, taking in the delicious scent.

"I've never smelled anything like this. Is there mint oil in it?" He asked.

She wasn't about to tell him she'd cast a spell on them both. "Yes, it's a little something extra I added. It makes the dish all the more special." She held the spoon out to him, and he took her by the wrist. His fingertips were cool to the touch. He held her hand for a few beats too long, and a flush warmed her chest and spread onto her cheeks. Could he see she was as pink as his roses? He stared into her eyes, his gaze holding hers far too long, and she hitched in her breath. Her mouth was so dry it was hard to swallow. He smiled, and as he leaned over for what she thought for certain was a kiss that would knock her flat on her ass, he opened his mouth and took the morsel of fruit into it. A sigh of relief burst from her lips. She wanted his kiss badly but she was terrified of it at the same time. She hadn't been with a man in several weeks, and none she had dated lately left her as weak in the knees as Tibor. The man controlled her waking dreams and lived in the shadows of her desire. She couldn't say no to him even if she wanted to ... and she didn't want to.

"It's delicious. I can't tell what fruit it is, though. I've never tasted anything like it."

She hoped to say she never tasted anything like him in an hour or two. "It's a lychee. They remind me of champagne."

"We'll have to compare them to the Moët. What other fruits are in your salad?"

"Here, try this." She aimed her spoon at the casserole but he reached out one hand and touched her wrist. Could he feel her pulse fluttering?

"No spoon. Your fingers. I want to taste it from you."

Her heart did a double-gainer flip. "Sure. I'd love to," she said softly. She dipped her index and middle finger into the dish and pulled out a scoop of salad. Tibor took her by the wrist and lifted her hand to his mouth. He parted his lips and her fingers slid inside. As he took the fruit into his mouth, he suckled on her fingers, tongue dancing between one fingertip and then the other, sucking as though he were making love to her hand. A bolt of desire shot from her solar plexus to her pussy. She warmed deep inside. She felt her nipples harden and she wondered what his lips would feel like wrapped around them. Oh, if his mouth was as talented as his fingers, she could only imagine how he would treat her most intimate spaces.

"You taste delicious," he said.

"What?" He startled her out of her daydream.

"You taste wonderful. Sweet with a hint of peppermint."

"That's my special oil. You also took in some blood orange and dragon fruit. I added maraschino cherries since you said you liked them." Her breath caught in her throat, and her voice squeaked as she spoke. Her skin warmed, despite a breeze flowing from the patio.

"You remembered I liked those cherries. I'm impressed. It takes a lot to impress me." He released her hand, and she almost whimpered in disappointment. Rather than wash her hands, she slipped her fingers into her mouth and smiled at him. His eyes flashed with desire, but he didn't take her in his arms the way she had hoped he would. Instead, he winked at her and walked back into the living room. She followed him to the couch, but he took her by the hand and pulled her towards the center of the room, taking her in his arms.

She lifted her head, ready for his kiss, but once again he did not lower his lips to hers. She knitted her eyebrows, confused over what he wanted, when he slipped one arm around her waist.

"Would you like to dance?" He wrapped his other arm around her back, and without missing a beat she rested her head against his broad chest. His heart thundered beneath her ear, revealing the arousal he hid so well from her. *So he's more aroused than he's letting on. He sure can keep a lid on his emotions. I wonder if I can do the same.*

They swayed to the slow beat of Clannad's lilting tune, and she shut her eyes to take in his closeness. Beneath the cedar and cinnamon lingered his masculine scent. His stubble brushed her forehead. Soft but firm lips pressed against her temple as they swayed to the music, and she gasped at the touch. She couldn't resist his barely-contained passion, but she froze, not wanting to appear too eager. She listened to the music and rocked back and forth, a gentle movement that only intensified her passion.

The air chilled around them as thunder crashed. The scent of amber intensified as if her magic has reached a crescendo. The sky darkened, casting shadows about her living room. The wind was a wild thing, blowing her pale blue linen curtains and rustling magazines sitting on her coffee table. Candle flames flickered as more shadows danced a fevered tarantella on her walls and ceiling. Fascinated, she watched as the shadows seemed to take on human form, writhing and spinning in an orgy against each other. A harbinger of things to come? A flash of lightning split the sky, and a moment later thunder crackled not far from her patio.

The storm was very close. Her curtains billowed in the wind, exhibiting the passion beneath her restrained dance with Tibor.

As a second fork of lightning flashed in the dark sky, she looked up to find her face inches from Tibor's. He lowered his head to hers and touched her lips with his own the moment thunder crashed around her home. Rain fell in hard sheets, but she didn't notice in the heat of his kiss. The feel of his mouth electrified her, unlike the men who slobbered all over her when they attempted the same. Why were some men such lousy kissers? Tibor knew what he was doing, and he expressed his kiss in a way that only made Sierra crave him more.

They stopped swaying and embraced each other, her desire so strong she couldn't resist his touch. She wanted to possess him, to feel as if their bodies entwined into one. He fisted her hair, pulled her head back and then planted his lips firmly against the pulse pounding in her throat. She moaned as more thunder crashed around them and rain pounded the ground. Lights flickered and went out. Clannad ground to a halt. They stood in the center of her living room, arms wrapped around each other, greeted only by a faint glow from the few candles that the wind hadn't blown out.

"We should shut your doors and windows."

Tibor's voice rasped with desire.

"Good idea." Her voice caught breathless in her throat. Although she resisted as much as she could, she pulled away from his embrace and raced to her French doors. Rain had fallen into her living room and she skidded on the floor, the near loss of balance making her heart leap even more. She closed the doors, and turned towards her windows to find Tibor closing them.

"Are there more open windows?"

"No. The ones upstairs are closed."

He smiled and laughed, a languid sound, and stared down at his clothing. "I'm drenched. I think I need a mop."

She looked down and saw her wet sweater and skirt stuck to her skin. "You're not the only one. I have a change of clothing for both of us. I always keep an extra set of men's and women's clothes handy for guests for emergencies like this."

He winked at her. "You have an extra set of men's clothing for all the men who visit you?"

"Stop teasing me. It's not like that." She snickered, since of course it was exactly like that, but she'd never met anyone like Tibor. Of all the men she entertained, and there were enough, Tibor set her heart aflame in ways the others couldn't even hold a candle to. "Follow me upstairs. I'll get a change of clothing for both of us. I can run your clothes through the dryer if you like."

"Thanks, I'd appreciate that."

"How would you like to sit on my deck and watch the storm? It's enclosed. The rain can't get it. Nature's brutality is an impressive thing to see." She said.

"I'd like that." He headed for the kitchen. "How about we take your delicious fruit salad and the champagne with us while we wait for the food to heat up?"

"Great idea. I'll get the bubbly."

Food and drink in hand, he followed behind her up the stairs to her bedroom, and she wondered if they'd actually change clothes and make it to the deck since her crisp sheets were only a few feet away. She had sprinkled lust magic powder on the soft cotton in the hours before he arrived, and she hoped her magic would inspire him. The food and champagne found their way to her dresser.

Tibor slipped out of his vest, ascot, and shirt, revealing a broad chest misted with black hair. Sierra hoped he didn't see her lick her lips. She took the clothing and dropped it in the dryer next to her bathroom. He slid out of his trousers and hung them on a hanger from her shower curtain. He stood before her dressed only in navy boxers. She wriggled out of her skirt and sweater, and in moments her clothes were tumbling in gentle heat next to Tibor's.

"You're not wearing a bra." His hoarse voice rumbled in her ears.

"I haven't worn one in twenty years."

She didn't resist when he placed one palm against her left breast and gave her a gentle squeeze. His breath hitched in. She stared at his face as he gazed into her eyes. How long could they keep up this dance? She wanted him in her bed, now, but she waited for him to make the moves.

He fondled her breasts with both hands. "You are, how do you say ... so firm, so ... perfect." She lowered her head and saw the tent in his boxers. He wanted her as much as she wanted him. "May I kiss them?"

He asked permission. How sweet. "Of course you may. I thought you'd never ask."

His lips brushed her nipples, and they hardened in response. He blew on them, making them so hard and sensitive they ached. His hands traveled down from her breasts to her bikini panties and he slid them down her legs. She stood naked before him, admiring the broad expanse of his shoulders. He swept her up in his arms and she laughed in astonishment as he carried her to her bed. The moment she had waited for all these months finally arrived, and her skin tingled at the feel of his arms wrapped around her, drawing rivulets of exquisite joy down her spine. They tossed back the comforter. The scent of amber and myrrh floated in a cloud around them as lightning cracked outside her deck, brightening the bedroom for a moment before going dark. Sierra saw the afterimage of Tibor's intense face as the brightness faded, giving him a devilish countenance. He seemed less than human, more a personification of pure vigor and animal lust as he took her. Thunder crackled around them, and the smell of ozone mingled with the amber and myrrh. She rested a hand on Tibor's bare chest only to feel a shock of static electricity jolt her out of her dream state. Sparks flew between them, literally and figuratively—little bolts of fairy light amid the darkness. Every grip of his hand to her arm, her breast, or her thigh exalted her, increasing her sensitivity to his touch.

His fingers found her sex and slid in without resistance. There was certainly no need for lube with him. She had been ready for him the moment she saw his beautiful nakedness. Moaning as she arched her back and stretched her legs, she closed her eyes while his fingers minueted inside her. The man knew just where to press and stroke to drive her into an erotic frenzy. Most men's fingers manhandled her, leaving her sore and unsatisfied, but Tibor's expert touch drove her into ecstasy. His thumb strummed her clit as he leaned over to kiss her left nipple. Wound so tightly she feared she'd burst, her climax came on more quickly than she expected. To her surprise, her long pent-up lust exploded and she thrashed beneath him, laughing with joy as she rode the crest of her own waves. His fingers didn't stop or slow down once as her orgasm overtook her. She bucked and thrashed and then curled into a ball in his arms, moaning in ecstasy the entire time.

"You came very quickly." Tibor said.

"Must be the company."

"I hope you aren't through yet."

"Not a chance."

"Good," he said as he pulled away. "Because I have plans."

She reached for him but he placed his index finger over her lips. He rose from the bed, grabbed the salad bowl, and returned to her side.

"Would you like to play?" he said in a teasing voice.

"Depends. What do you have in mind?"

"How about this?" He scooped a bit of fruit onto the spoon and dropped it onto over her right nipple. He did the same to her left nipple. The confection chilled her, and her nipples hardened at the cold. Tibor lowered his head and nibbled at the dragon fruit and blood orange slices a little at a time, not rushing his attention. He languished against her breasts, licking her right nipple and then her left, until she could have melted in a puddle beneath him. She took in a few deep breaths to overcome the rush of adrenaline that coursed through her body. She wanted to run with him, to free herself from the ordinariness of her days and enjoy the company of this delicious man.

She placed a hand on his shoulder to turn him over so she could give him the pleasure he was giving her, but he held his fingers against her lips again. Thunder crackled overhead as a torrent of rain battered her windows. The storm gave an urgency to their lovemaking, and she eagerly awaited his next move. Giving her a broad grin, he reached for the salad and fingered a lychee. He plopped it on her navel, and then ran it down her belly until it hovered over her pussy. The heat emanating from her sex warmed her entire body. Waves crashed against the rocks beyond her home as if ocean sprites encouraged her to lose herself in Tibor's embrace. Cymopoleia, the Greek goddess of storms, spoke to her through the pummeling rain, telling her to let Tibor do whatever he wanted and to follow his lead.

Shadows cast on her ceiling from candlelight writhed and twisted in their erotic dance. She closed her eyes and relaxed her body, waiting for his next move. Cool fruit and sour cream chilled her pussy and thighs as Tibor dabbed more of the salad against her skin. Even though she knew what was coming, the moment his tongue touched her pussy lips she groaned with pleasure. He lapped at her folds, growing more intense with each lick. As he ate her out he moaned with delight, making her giggle. Ticklish, she writhed beneath him, but he held her fast by grasping her arms at her wrists and holding her in place. He worked his magic as he licked and sucked, and her heart raced with excitement. She wanted to get lost in her fever dream, to feel his tongue wrap around her soul, to feel him deep inside her, thrusting until she could take the pressure no longer. Waves crashed in time with the beat of her racing heart, and lightning shined upon his wild face, bringing forth the animal that lurked within. As she gazed into his eyes, an orgasm more powerful than her last shook her body. She gripped him tightly as she came, closing her eyes to take in the full effect of her climax.

She stood on the beach as the Nor'easter bellowed around her. Her legs weren't wet although waves crashed about her as high as her calves, but she paid no mind to how odd that was. How did she get out here? Where was Tibor? Disoriented, she gazed into the storm. As she took a few steps into the surf, a lilting voice sang in the distance. That voice had lured ships and men to their deaths close to the rocks not far from shore. Norwich's coastline claimed numerous shipwrecks, all drawn by the power of that seductive voice. It was especially dangerous to be at sea during a storm like this. Most ships waited out a Nor'easter, but this tempest hovered on the edge of mystery and enchantment. Lightning forked across the angry sky, casting a glow upon dark clouds flowing through a mist in the distance. Thunder crashed around her moments later, but she felt serene and safe knee-deep in water that didn't drench her for some strange reason.

A hazy figure approached her through the mist. Fear tapped at her spine as it drew near. Should she turn around and leave? She turned and saw nothing but water surrounding her without land in sight. When did she drift so far from shore? She feared walking because she didn't know which way led to land. She could walk further out to sea without knowing it and drown. Her head spun in confusion. Why was the water up to her waist? Her body rocked back and forth as the waves pummeled her. The opaque ocean hid monsters and sea serpents beneath its whitecaps, and Sierra's heart thumped in terror.

The figure of a woman materialized through the mist two yards away, standing a full three feet taller than Sierra. She floated on the whitecaps as if she were a part of them. Seaweed hair blew about in the wind, braiding and unbraiding as it draped over her sharp shoulders. Scales covered the tops of her sea green arms and her full breasts. To Sierra's astonishment, the woman had no navel, something that fascinated her in her dream state. This woman was not born. She was a child of the sea, and Sierra recognized her.

"Cymopoleia." She whispered.

The woman opened her mouth and seawater and snails fell out. Her eyes blinked from side to side, not up and down as humans' do. She extended one arm, hand outstretched in warning.

"Don't let him leave you tonight." Her voice thundered like the rain, echoing in the mist.

"What?"

"Don't let him leave you tonight. The ocean is a raging beast that will swallow him whole. It cares not for human emotion, want, or need. It takes what it wants."

Apprehension crawled up Sierra's spine. She knew better than to ignore Cymopoleia's warning. The storm around her seemed more furious than what bellowed around her home. Where was she, and how did she get all the way out here surrounded by waist-deep water?

"Take heed of my words." Caution colored the goddess's voice. "Do not let him leave you tonight. That is my gift to you."

Sierra awakened with a start, relieved to feel her cheek against her pillow. She patted her body to find it dry. Bed sheets cocooned her, damp only in her sweat and Tibor's. She smelled his rugged scent beneath the tang of salt and surf.

"That must have been some dream." Tibor said as he scratched her back.

"I fell asleep?" She curled into his fingers, relishing the feel of his nails across her skin.

"You passed out. You had the orgasm to end all orgasms and then you collapsed."

"I'm sorry. I had no idea I fell asleep."

"I took it as a complement. I must have had quite an effect on you for you to sleep so soundly. Did you know you snore?"

She sat up, thinking about what the goddess of storms had said to her. Sierra often honored and prayed to Cymopoleia, especially lately since it often rained, but she had never encountered the goddess before. Why this time of all times?

Lightning lit up her bedroom. The storm thundered around her. She looked at her clock to see numbers flash.

"The power's back on." She said. "We can turn on the lights."

"I rather like watching you by candlelight. It's more romantic."

So he liked romance? It wasn't all about fucking for him, something she had hoped was the case before he entered her home. The man danced with her, so he definitely enjoyed a magical aura to his relationships. He seemed to hail from another era, with the way he dressed, his manner of speech, and his dreamy way of enjoying their date.

"I had a strange dream." Sierra said.

"A nightmare?" Tibor asked. "Want to tell me about it?"

"No, it's okay. It wasn't a nightmare. Just bizarre. I was standing in the middle of the ocean. I don't remember much beyond that." She didn't want to discuss it with him. Telling him about it would make it seem too real.

"As long as you're okay. I don't want you to feel uneasy for any reason."

"I don't feel uneasy at all, especially with you around." She kicked away the swaddling sheets and scooted backwards until she sat with her back against her headboard. "Enough about bad dreams. I want to know more about you. You're from Budapest?" She asked.

"Yes. My family has lived there for generations."

"So how did you end up in Massachusetts?"

"I work for an engineering company that sent me here for six months. I'm working at the American branch. It's much different from Hungary."

"I can imagine." Her heart sank. Only six months? She'd already wasted two of those months dancing around him at the local Stop 'n' Shop. She needed to make the most of his remaining time in Norwich. "How do you like it here?"

"I love it. I bought a resident parking sticker so I may visit your beaches when it warms up."

"It's been very warm for this time of year. Have you been to the beach yet?"

"Yes, twice, but not to this beach. It's beautiful here, even in the middle of a thunderstorm and a power outage."

"Get use to the power outages. They happen a lot here during storms. We also get flooding and the occasional tornado."

"I hope your lovely home doesn't flood."

"No, thank God. I'm elevated enough that the flood waters tend to go further away to the roads a couple of miles down the coast."

"You mean Atlantic Road? I drove that way to get here. It's the shortest route and it's quite scenic."

A flash of lightning illuminated her bedroom. Thunder rumbled outside, battering the clouds and crackling against the sky. Rain fell in steady sheets against her windows.

"I wish I could go to your beach now, but the

weather won't allow it," he said.

"My deck is enclosed. We can sit out there if you like. Storms at sea are impressive."

He rose naked from the bed and walked to the door to the deck. Candlelight enhanced his beautiful form, casting shadows against his flexing muscles. He was right—turning on the lights would cast too harsh a glare on their magical and romantic evening together. Candlelight set the right alluring mood.

He turned towards her and gave her a warm smile. "You can get the deck ready. I'll get our champagne."

In moments they stood on the deck and champagne bubbled in Sierra's glasses. Thick pillar candles burned on every table, giving the room an enchanting glow. Tibor stood in front of her bookcase, holding a thick, leather-bound tome. He leafed through some pages. He held her family's Book Of Shadows, spells her mother and grandmother had written. She swallowed hard, fearing his reaction to her truth. How much should she tell him? Although she knew little about him, she trusted him and wanted him to accept her for who she was.

"Interesting book. Is this a book of spells?" he asked.

This was as good a time as any to tell him about her family's legacy. Nervous, she shifted from one foot to the other, hoping as she spoke that he would not grab his clothes and flee for her front door. "Yes, that's a spell book. I inherited that book from my mother. She got it from my grandmother." Although she feared he would scoff at her family's legacy or—worse—reject her, she admitted the truth. "I practice ocean magic. My mother and grandmother taught me. We're a family of witches."

He paused, and she waited for the worst. "You're a witch? I've never met a witch before."

"I own a small Wiccan shop downtown and a second one in Salem."

"Salem, where the women and one man accused of witchcraft were hanged?"

"Yes. Well, the women were hanged. Giles Corey was pressed to death. They were innocent, but now the city is full of witches. Its nickname is Witch City. There are occult shops all over the place there." She smiled. "The irony is not lost on me."

He put the book back into the bookcase. Although two Adirondack chairs stood directly behind her, he sat on the large wooden swing and then patted the seat next to him. She took the hint and raced to his side to sit down. He wrapped his arm around her as both of them sat naked taking in the storm that roared around them. Lightning flashed far out at sea, forks slamming the ocean's surface.

"You can imagine I'm skeptical," he said.

"I understand. It might be a bit hard to take in. I don't cast curses or anything like that, though."

"I figured if you did, you'd have good reason," he said. "Do you cast spells?"

"Yes."

He grinned. "Love spells?"

She grinned back. "Yes."

"Did you cast one on me?"

"No." It was the truth. "I did cast a few spells to make our evening memorable, though."

"So that's why your sheets smells so good. The perfume is a spell?"

"Yes. You smelled amber. Amber is associated with romance. There's also myrrh but that's a seasonal fragrance I like."

"Your spell worked. This evening certainly has been magical." He ran his fingers through her hair. "I approve."

A sigh of relief burst from her lips. She leaned into his body, making herself comfortable. "I hoped you would."

"So tell me about ocean magic."

She fought for words, but they wouldn't come. Then, she realized the best way to explain her gifts to him. "Rather than tell you, I'd like to show you."

She stood and walked to the windows facing the

ocean. Rain pelted the glass. "Don't be alarmed by what you see. Ocean magic can be powerful. It's a bit overwhelming the first time you see it."

"I'm ready for anything," he said. "I'd like to see what you have to offer. I'm fascinated."

Good. He's attentive. Now to hope this display doesn't scare him to death. "Watch the ocean." Lowering her head, she took a few deep breaths to clear her mind. As she arched her back she shook out her arms to relax them in preparation for what she was about to do. She reached out and placed her hands against the window. The coolness of the glass chilled her palms. Since Cymopoleia saw fit to speak to her in her dream, she chose to address the goddess. She muttered under her breath. "Oh, dearest Cymopoleia, goddess of storms, would you please be so kind as to come for a visit? Please show us your power, if you so wish."

The air thickened around her, and a few candles blew out. Lightning streaked across the sky, illuminating the roiling surface of the ocean. The water emitted a pale glow like seaglass catching sunlight several hundred yards out to sea, and soon grew in intensity as the light pulsed amid the waves. Churning as if caught in a mad boil, the water erupted as strange shapes rose from the depths. Sierra watched Tibor's reflection in the glass as he rose from the swing. Her arms ached with the pressure of holding onto the window.

A mast rose from the deep, and then a second and third followed. Tattered sails bustled in the maelstrom as a ship grew out of the dark water. The galleon rocked on the angry sea, glowing the color of seafoam. Sparks jumped in a Saint Vitus Dance along the masts. The sound of wood creaking mixed with the roar of the wind. It was only fitting that Cymopoleia would reveal a ship she sank herself.

Tibor stood beside her, gaping at the spectacle. She turned briefly to see a look of astonishment and a little fear cross his rugged face.

"What is that?" His voice was so quiet she barely heard him.

"One of the lost ships. I don't know which one. Norwich has its share of shipwrecks." Her arms ached from pressing her palms so hard against the glass, holding back the storm writhing only a few feet from them. "I can't hold it anymore." She dropped her arms to her sides. Immediately, the phantom ship collapsed in trillions of rain droplets and fell into the sea.

Tibor said nothing. Sierra rubbed the cramp out of her arms, and waited for him to say something. Anything.

"I don't know what to say," he whispered.

Say you aren't afraid of me. "I know. I don't show something like that to people often, but when I do, they're dumbfounded."

"Why did you choose to show it to me?"

Her heart thumped with anxiety as she revealed herself to him. "Because I trust you. And I like you. I took a chance with you, and I hope I made the right decision."

He smiled at placed a hand on her shoulder. "You did. I'm speechless, and that's rare for me."

She flexed her hands, working away the stiffness. "I hope I didn't scare you. I'm really quite harmless." She turned to him, but he wouldn't look at her. He only stared out to sea, searching amid the waves. Was he looking for more magic? "I usually cast protection spells and read tarot cards, although I've never been able to read my own future. I'm not good at that."

"You can read cards?" He turned to her and squeezed her shoulder, not holding back his eagerness. Her body eased into his touch, happy at his attention. "I haven't had a card reading done since I was a child." He smiled at her. "My grandmother used to read them. She was quite good."

"Did I put you out?"

"I don't understand what you mean—what is 'put out'?"

She swallowed hard, nervous. "Did I scare you?"

"A little." He placed a hand on her shoulder, and she took his hand in hers. "I've never seen anything like that before. You sure you don't cast curses?"

She giggled, still nervous. "No, I haven't had a need to. Would you like me to read cards for you?"

His smile crinkled the corners of his eyes. She relaxed a little, since he seemed to be warming to her again. "I'd love that. You surprise me, Sierra. You're a very exciting woman."

She took him by the hand and guided him back to the swing. "It's too dark in here. Let me light some candles. Watch me. You'll get a kick out of this."

He sat and she walked to a dark red pillar and blew on the wick. The flame sparked to life. Tibor laughed. She turned to smile at him, walked to the next candle, and blew the flame alive. His smile lit up his face.

"You amaze me. I've never met anyone quite like you. You're magical in more ways than one."

"I need some champagne," she said. "That little trick with the ship took a lot out of me." She sat on the swing next to him as he poured champagne for them both. Lightning forked against the clouds far out at sea, reaching for the heavens and crashing against the waves.

"That show was very impressive, but this storm is impressive all by itself. Your view is incredible. I've never seen a storm at sea before," he said. "It's rained near my home but I've never seen anything like this."

"This is a typical Nor'easter. They're intense and perfect for spending time indoors enjoying a meal by candlelight."

"And other things." He grinned.

She giggled in agreement. "You're right about that. So you're okay with me now?"

"I've never not been okay with you."

"Good. I hope you keep coming back. I know you aren't far away. You live in Rockport?" Rockport was the coastal town about 20 miles south of Norwich.

"Yes, in mid-town in a 200 year old rental. I love it. Living in this area is like going back in time."

"Norwich and Rockport do have that other-era quality about them. In winter they look like a Currier and Ives painting when it snows."

"I know who they are. My family sends me Christmas cards with those paintings on the front." He patted her shoulder, and in response she curled her body into his. Tension left her as she realized he wasn't going to flee her home in terror knowing who and what she was. They relaxed in the swing and sipped champagne for several minutes in silence, listening to the call of the storm. Sierra felt at peace, secure in knowing Tibor would not leave her.

Sirens howled in the distance and grew louder as they approached her home. Red and blue lights flashed past her windows. The sirens dopplered to a lower pitch as the ambulance and police crew sped down the road.

Curious, Sierra stood up and walked to her stereo. "I wonder what that's all about?" She turned on the radio and turned the knob to a local station. "The news here is pretty quick. There might be a report already about what's going on."

Static crackled from the speakers and a deep voice spoke. "... flooding along the Rowley and Norwich coast leading into Innsmouth. Police report a single car accident on Atlantic Road two miles south of Norwich at the Old Cape Beach Bridge, which has been destroyed by heavy rain. The inhabitants of the car are presumed washed out to sea. Helicopter crews are scanning the area looking for survivors. The road has collapsed in severe flooding. Gale force winds, heavy rain and flood warning in effect until 10 am tomorrow morning. Please remain indoors and do not drive except in the event of an emergency. Avoid Atlantic Road until further notice ..."

A chill descended over Sierra. "Didn't you say you took Atlantic Road to get here?"

"Yes." His quiet voice couldn't hide his unease. "I remember crossing that bridge. The tide was so high it was almost up to the road around it. I'd have taken that route to get home."

Sierra understood Cymopoleia's warning.

Although she feared his reaction, she felt an urgent need to tell Tibor about her dream. "Well, you've seen my books. You saw the galleon. I told you I practice ocean magic. I didn't tell you the truth when I said I couldn't remember much of my dream. I remember it very vividly." She paused to swallow, but her dry throat only clenched with anxiety. "It was about you."

"How? What did you dream?"

"I saw a goddess I've been familiar with for a long time. She's a storm goddess, and her Greek name is Cymopoleia. She's the one I called to give you that little demonstration at sea. This is the first time she ever appeared to me. She told me to not let you leave my home tonight."

Tibor blinked a few times. Sierra saw the trepidation on his face. "So you think I would have tried to cross that bridge and possibly drowned in the ocean?"

"Seems obvious enough to me."

"I wouldn't have believed it if I hadn't seen your magic in action myself. This is very unnerving. I'm grateful to you for the warning. And to your goddess. It's very unsettling. I think you need to hold me now and make me feel better." He smiled at her, clearly taking advantage of his situation.

She walked to him and wrapped her arms around him. His arms hugged her back, and she felt secure in his embrace. When she lifted her head, he smiled at her again and lowered his face to hers. Their lips touched, first with hesitation, and then with passion to intense she melted in his arms. Their kiss blossomed into the passion she felt for him as her tongue found his. He tasted of coconut, exotic fruit, and mint. His manly scent floated around her, making her so dizzy she clung to him fearing she'd topple over in her excitement. Her head spun as his tongue explored her mouth. How long had she craved a man who attended to her every need and lusted after her as much as she lusted after him? Had it been weeks? Months? No man she had dated thus far could match Tibor in the rugged manhood department. He felt comfortable in his body and it showed in the way he kissed her and made love to her. She liked a man who enjoyed himself.

When was the last time she trusted a man so fully as to show him her power? Despite not knowing him well, something about Tibor urged her to reveal herself to him. She took a chance, and he responded well to her. She couldn't let him get away from her, especially since she could so easily have lost him to the sea.

She glanced at the clock and saw that only a short time had passed since he had arrived on her doorstep. "Are you hungry? I think dinner is warm enough by now, even with the blackout. The oven holds heat very well."

"I'm starving. That little ocean display gave me an appetite. Your fruit salad was incredible but I need a meal for sustenance."

She took him by the hand and guided him from her deck and into her living room, pausing on the way to pick up the fruit salad. Both of them were stark naked. She placed the salad on the dining room table, and gave him a sweet smile. As she walked around the dining room table and blew the flames onto the extinguished candles, Tibor's eyes widened in astonishment and he smiled with approval. Once their plates were full of his exquisite Hungarian food, she set them on her table. Tibor took his seat, waiting for her. But, instead of sitting beside him, Sierra walked to her coffee table to grab her favorite tarot deck before returning to the dinner table. It was a deck depicting cats of exotic breeds. She loved cats. Her own puss slept in his bed in her living room, oblivious to the storm. Once the meal was finished, she would introduce him to Tibor. She took a seat at the head of the table away from their plates, and called Tibor over.

"Let me read a spread for you, since you asked, and then one for us. I love reading the tarot. This way, we can look into our futures and decide how we want to go about things." She laid out a spread of cards. "But first, let's have more of my fruit salad. It's given us good luck so far this evening."

She spooned some oranges and maraschino cherries into his mouth, and he closed his eyes as the juice burst onto his tongue, a contented smile unfurling across his handsome face. Sitting back, happy and serene, her upcoming days looked bright and full of magic. She might never have been good at reading her own future, but she had confidence that the future held only love and passion for her and Tibor.

The Cherry Orchard

A Steampunk Fairy Tale

Vanessa de Sade

The Cherry Orchard

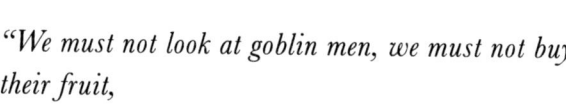

"We must not look at goblin men, we must not buy their fruit,
Who knows upon what soil they fed, their hungry, thirsty root."

– Christina Rossetti (Goblin Market)

Chapter One

Magda and Victor

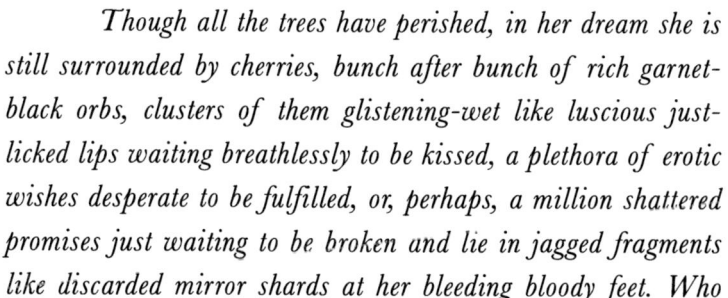

Though all the trees have perished, in her dream she is still surrounded by cherries, bunch after bunch of rich garnet-black orbs, clusters of them glistening-wet like luscious just-licked lips waiting breathlessly to be kissed, a plethora of erotic wishes desperate to be fulfilled, or, perhaps, a million shattered promises just waiting to be broken and lie in jagged fragments like discarded mirror shards at her bleeding bloody feet. Who could tell?

And even when she wakes—naked, sweat-drenched and panting, her heart pounding like an overcharged defibrillator—she can still taste them sweet and sickly in her mouth, their purple-black sap pungent, almost bittersweet, on her own dry lips.

And, strange though it might seem, her future seems to lie before her in that magical forest, all her expectations contained in the waxy, glossy fruit, just waiting to burst open anew and awaken the forgotten sensations that she feels have atrophied centuries before ...

―――――◇◇◇―――――

No one remembers the old Paris. The iron tower remains, of course, or what's left of it, at any rate. Though Magda doesn't much like it. It reminds her of her dreams, she says, with its mangled metal arms reaching vainly into the white cloudless sky like a mad woman writhing in a gray bed, or the sea when the storm winds come to gobble up more and more chunks of the fragile coastline, whole cliff faces and even cities crumbling into the boiling cauldron that is now the ocean.

The Party denies it all of course, saying that reports of The Erosion are greatly exaggerated, but Magda, a State Cartographer and no dumb bunny to boot, knows better, though she keeps her seditious opinions quietly to herself. Her position has given her access to some of the New Republic's oldest atlases in the restricted rooms of the great windowless library on the *Rue de Celeste*, hefty leather-bound volumes that smell of salt spray and dried grasses, heavy as a sleeping child and bigger than her straining arms; yet she pores lovingly over them daily and reads them like adventure stories, seeing not tables of crop allocations or pestilence barriers, but the living contours of the great mountain ranges of the north, their snowy peaks immense like great white breasts arising from the fertile body of the old earth; or the vast immeasurable oceans, mighty like speckled mares pawing angrily against their landlocked halters.

Today, though, it is Saturday and she heads not to her allocated place of employment but to the Automation House of Madame Augustine. An old nineteenth century mansion which slumps sleepily on the steep slope on what is left of the *Rue Montmarte*, tucked neatly into the shadow of the shattered black tower of the now derelict Ministry of Aviation building, and invisible to the prying eyes of patrol ships as they sail majestically by above, great ocean liners of the sky with their long observation decks and glinting brass telescopes silently observing an annotating.

Magda especially likes this particular Automaton House because Madame does not charge in credits, preferring instead the soft warmth of the antique copper Centimes of the Old Order which can still be bartered for Food Tokens from the Carpet Baggers on the Boulevards, hasty exchanges made in the cat-pee-scented shadows of the dry bridges in the wake of the Patrols, everyone still alert for silent whales creeping menacingly across the polished platinum of the noonday skies.

Sun goggles are issued with glass that is a bright ocher-orange verging on red nowadays, making the blistering pavements look like pock-marked kiln-fired terracotta, but they hurt Magda's eyes and she still prefers her ancient set of ex-military issue in a cool green, turning the stifling noonday streets into soft undersea cycloramas, the passing Damsels in their summer frocks and high-piled hair ornaments like fecund mermaids beckoning her into their coral-flower bowers.

And a Patrol Ship passes soundlessly by now as she strides boldly along the *Rue Montmarte*, momentarily blotting out the burning sun with its lumbering bulk, a huge verdigrised behemoth in tarnished copper, myriads of dials and levers swirling in a perpetual symphony of brass cogs and steel rivets, a humming analogue beehive unceasingly cataloging everyone's every move, the blank-eyed faces of the Observers on the viewing decks expressionless as they identify her and record her locale, the thin spidery masts at the rear of the ship beaming all their data soundlessly back to the whirring calculation units in Party Central.

Not that visiting Automation Houses is technically illegal, of course, and with the shortage of fertile men after the Second Great Pestilence, even the Party Stalwarts have been forced to turn a blind eye to their existence, acknowledging in secret memorandums that they do, in fact, form an integral part of maintaining discipline in the Republic. But it is still not good to have too many visits to them recorded on your files, and many a Citizen has been transported to the Mutant Zones on the strength of an Excessive Decadence charge, an attached record of credits cashed at establishments of ill repute being sufficient evidence to uphold the order.

So, breathing like a lonely deep sea diver in her private subterranean world, Magda, resplendent in her best Dandy suit, stops and quickly stoops on one knee, ostensibly taking care of an unlaced boot, until the great air vessel sails by above her and then counts to sixty, as she has been taught, clearing the range of the viewing deck's data sweep, and then, rising, darts like a quicksilver fish into the softly curtained vestibule of Madame's domain.

And, at first, she can see nothing in the womb-like gloom, her flinty blue eyes sun-blinded despite the green goggles and the visor of her neat brown derby. But then, gradually, as she unfastens her ocular protection, her vision become accustomed to the gloom, and she discerns the padded doorway to her place of enchantment behind the thick and all-enveloping red velvet drapes.

Madame has her usual room ready, a modest chamber on the third floor with carpet on the floor and old sepia photographs of naked women on the walls. And though many of the ladies who patronize this house question the very existence of all the female pornography on its walls, Magda finds a quiet pleasure in studying these softly arousing images while she's being fucked. Not for erotic stimulation, *per se*, or even for the body comparison that some of her friends indulge in, weighing up the heavy udder-like bosoms of those long-dead courtesans against their own little bubs as the Automatons tirelessly service their aching cunts. No, Magda finds no stimulation in competition, but there is, nevertheless, a hunger in her for the stories that these concupiscent images have to tell.

Today, for example, she regards a heavy-hipped voluptuary who stands preening into the camera, naked save for her new ostrich feather hat and gleaming leather lace-up ankle boots, a luxuriant fur wrap draped casually over a chair in the background and expensive clothing strewn upon the freshly polished floor. Her breasts are pert and pointy, stomach and thighs rounded and nubile, and her cunt shaved smooth and her slit obvious. Ah, men's cocks must have risen like the morning tide, Magda muses, following the curves and contours of all that exposed labia as though it were a map in her place of work, visualizing the eager tongues which would have flicked and teased at the almost certainly large clit that nestled just out of sight of the camera's probing lens. No wonder clients lavished furs and velvets upon this Victorian Venus, sucking on her pointy little tits like hungry piglets at the teat, impatient to push their big slippery cocks up inside her, coming like tropical geysers within seconds of being admitted to that most holy of valleys, vying amongst each other for her hand and her heart, all of them rich with promises of bonbons and apartments on the *Champs Élysée* where they would keep her, secret and hidden, a brightly-colored butterfly fluttering on the pin of their outward respectability. No wonder she mocked them with her laughing eyes and elfish grin.

And Magda has come many times, visualizing herself as that fulsome woman, long gone yet not forgotten.

Today, though, she has little time for daydreaming, for the urge is strong upon her and she selects the biggest and most robust of the Automations for her purpose. Madame smiles knowingly when Magda makes her choice and quietly whispers a sum in her ear, and, though there is a momentary hesitation,

Magda nods and delves into her pocket for the requisite Centimes, passing the warm copper coins to Madame in a seamless fluid movement, as if they were both still out in the street with the Patrol Ships hovering overhead.

"Your usual room, Chérie?" the older woman asks in an accent that bears no resemblance to French, but Magda nods and plays her part. And thus we find her, on this stiflingly hot Saturday afternoon, in that little airless chamber on the third floor, impatient and already naked, waiting for her paramour.

And, though some say that Madame's Automations lack the rough masculinity of those of other houses, with their Marcel-waved hair, fine features and soft latex skin, Magda finds them long-running and insistent, their jerky clockwork cocks molded exquisitely into a permanent state of arousal and fitted with small vibrational units that rub oh so softly on your clit; plus, beneath the surface, there are intricate Swiss watch-maker's mechanisms that skilfully delay ejaculation until they feel the tight clench of pussy muscles well absorbed in the throes of climaxing.

But now a Maid brings the machine that has been ordered and she looks approvingly at Magda's denuded body, while straightening imaginary creases in the bedding. "This is Victor," she says by way of introduction. "He has been fully wound and will be everything you have ordered, Miss, possibly even more. Enjoy!" And she trails a soft hand imperceptibly over the curve of Magda's alabaster behind as she leaves, a wistful look in her eyes.

"Good day, Magda," Victor sing-songs in his slightly too-high voice, like an antique clockwork nightingale trilling in its golden cage, and there is only a tiny—almost indiscernible—pause between his stock greeting and her name, a tiny click as the delicate jeweled gears in his voice box seamlessly select the correct identifier disc. "Which position do you require for satisfaction today?"

And Magda smiles at his directness. She has heard tales of a machine in the brothels of Buenos Aries which can actually hold a conversation and seduce its users, but none of Madame's robots are capable of such subtlety.

"I think, from behind, today, Victor, dear. Hard but not fast," she says without blushing and the Automation nods, his chest almost girlish in its smoothness but his cock huge and lubricated, making Magda swallow with desire and experience a shiver all over her naked body.

She had tried to suck the stiff prick of one of the love machines once, many years ago, filled with a romantic desire to swallow all its thick, tapioca-starch semen, but, though it had looked real, the substantial blue-veined member had tasted only of lubricant, and she had sunk back onto the softness of the bed, pouting and unsatisfied, opening her legs wide in invitation and clawing at his cold body as he pounded steadily into her hot pussy, splitting her open like a soft peach in summer.

Today, though, with the urge strong in her, she has no fanciful needs and quickly bends over on all fours on the narrow bed for Victor's purpose. She is a tall girl of around twenty-nine years in the conventional calendar, with long and athletic legs and a firm well-sculpted bottom—peachy someone once called it in some other life— and her cunt is an Aladdin's cave of pleasure which yawns like an open secret, all her sugar pink and ruby red petals on show to the Machine's appraising eye.

"Do you require manual stimulation?" Victor asks with a slight catch in his voice as his hand traces the damp folds of her pussy, and runs a finger slowly up her ass crack, circling her little pinky-brown starfish, but Magda shakes her head.

"Not today, Victor, I'm too horny, just fuck me," she whispers through gritted teeth and the machine immediately obliges, his big cock expertly nosing its way into her wet and slippery crack until the huge plum-like head is submerged, pausing only momentarily until he feels her vaginal muscles grip him, then he gives a gentle push and slides right in up to the hilt, his large firm hands gripping her hips as he begins to build a slow, insistent rhythm.

"That's right, fuck me like that," Magda pants, grinding her sleek ass up into him to anticipate his thrusts. "Now harder, but don't speed up, just keep that same pace but really push your cock into me and make my pussy yearn for you. Yes, that's it, that's it … Yes, harder, harder, harder. Yes, yes, yes …"

There are several thousand finely-crafted brass cogs inside the machine that is Victor, and a hundred million glittering gem stones ensure that each tiny twirling wheel is perfectly balanced, all of his several hundred flawlessly articulated joints moving in syncopated rhythm as he hard-fucks Magda to orgasm, his light, bird-like voice whispering her name again and again as he pounds and thrusts, a tiny heat unit inside him warming his artificial seminal fluid to just the right pitch before he speeds up and hammers into her, the hot jism shooting out of the tiny gaping hole in his pulsing member like a burst hydrant and filling her up just like a good boy should.

And she feels him coming just as her own orgasm begins to abate, then feels the familiar dry itch inside her tighten up and convulse again, and before she knows what has hit her she being tossed on a tidal wave of pleasure once more, this second helping of sensations even more earth-shattering than the first, Victor's firm hands still holding her thrusting hips in check like a wild piebald mare he's breaking, matching her frantic pace in a way no living man could do and still pushing into her, harder, harder, harder until he utters a strange half mangled shout and comes again, a first for a machine, all his delicate clockwork joints grinding with effort as he pounds his huge prick mercilessly into her slit, saying her name over and over again until he finally runs out of wind and slumps down beside her as she lies back, sweat-drenched, thrilling to the sound of her own iron heart pounding in her ears.

Chapter Two

Cynthia and Grandmamma

One dreamy day, at the end of childhood, Grandmamma takes Magda to the theatre.

She has just turned eighteen and has celebrated her coming-of-age by having all her luxuriant golden hair bobbed into a neat razor-sharp fringe.

And though her birthday gifts that morning have included three new rainbow-hued flapper frocks in fashionably short lengths; a string of clickety-clack amber beads that glow with a phosphorescent fire when you hold them to your eye; and a gramophone with a big brass horn and pearlescent teak-wood cabinet to hold her records, it was the trip to the West End which still stuck in her mind all these years later. The journey in the taxi cab through the rain-slaked streets;

London, learning to sing again, stretching its arms like a sleeper awakened after the long drab years of the Great War; the bustling department stores laden with treasures; the crowds surging along Oxford Street; the shouting newsboys on all the corners; and the lights, oh the lights, of Piccadilly Circus.

They had all had supper at Simpsons on the Strand and then taken up their box at the Empire, a big gold-encrusted bower which nestled among the old theater's giant crystal chandeliers, high above the rest of the audience who scurried around in the stalls below them like ermined ants, their furs and jewels winking in the klieg lights reflected glow.

Crowned heads of countries long-forgotten had sat where they now sat, and famed thespians from Garrick to Irving had taken their bows and then smiled up in their direction. And tonight they had come to see *The Cherry Orchard*, the first real play that Magda had ever been invited to attend. She had been to the circus and the pantomime many times before, of course, but these flimsies were mere vaudevilles for children and tonight was different; tonight was *theatre* and here she was resplendent in shimmering silk and in the best box in the house, the entire audience peering up at her through their gleaming brass and mother-of-pearl opera glasses, conjecturing on what daughter of what crowned head this little debutant was with her neatly cut hair and scintillating amber necklace.

And, crowning glory, on her lap, in a beribboned red and white candy-striped box from the best *bonboniere* in Bond Street, was a casket of Matinee Selection, lush pastes and marzipans shaped to resemble luscious cherries hand-tinted in blush pinks and chrome yellows and soaked in kirsch and maraschino; fat sugarplum damsons in the darkest purples and indigos, liqueur-steeped and sweeter than butterfly wings and summer wine. Grandmamma always said that chocolates were vulgar and suited only to middle class taste, and that the true confectioner's art lay solely in nuts and pastes. And so, even from their earliest days, she had always brought them candied fruits fat as waxy gems; brightly colored boxes of San Toy selection from nights at Daly's; and Arabian almonds coated in brittle sugar shells and tinted in the palest pastel pinks or robin's-egg blues.

And tonight the rush from the alcohol in the bonbons going straight to her head, and her little heart, delirious with happiness, is pitter-pattering like a pecking-chicken-toy by the time the house lights finally go down and the gas jets in the huge brass spotlights flare to an icy blue hiss and illuminate the sedately rising red velvet curtain and the great Russian dacha set that waits beyond.

The program in her hand has stated that

tonight's play is to be a comedy, but that inadequate word conveys nothing of the great depth of feeling that this intricate work will present. And Magda watches, breathless, with tears in her bright blue eyes as she shares the agony of Madame Ranevskaya and her family as their estate and entire way of life slips through their blasé fingers like warm sand on a summer day at the beach; yet, when the final curtain falls on the poor stooped figure of Firs, the faithful old butler, abandoned by the family and entombed to die in the now derelict château, her whole body shakes with unconcealed rage at the cold-blooded callousness of her own privileged class.

"Did you like the play, my dear?" her grandmother asks as they emerge, gasping and out of breath, into the tinderbox aroma of the rain-washed London streets, hansom cabs and taxis vying for their trade in the hiss of gaslight, and Magda grasps the older woman's wrists and whispers, "It has changed my life," little realizing how prophetic this statement will be.

And thus the interminable Season and that long hot summer drags on, with London society blissfully unaware that the First Great Pestilence will soon sweep across Europe and decimate almost the whole of her population in a matter of weeks.

Party membership is also on the up, with shipyard workers striking in the streets and the great Stepney docks lying idle, rusted hulks with rotting cargos becalmed up and down the hot, foetid waters of the sluggish Thames.

Magda, meanwhile, has also joined The Party—secretly, of course—and she is sending most of her generous allowance to help boost their scanty funds, though she has not yet adopted the austere mode of dress favored by some of her contemporaries, and she still glitters with the lightning-white fire of diamonds when she accompanies her Grandmamma to the Opera—but she is a quieter, more earnest girl than that tipsy young Deb so affected by a Chekhov play in what already seems like another life.

And tonight is the night of her own cotillion and she stands resplendent in the Savoy ballroom before the cream of London society in a shimmering pearl sheath dress that clings to her slender body like skin, a tall and athletic girl with hair the color of wild primroses, bobbed and razor-fringed, naked save for the million sparkling tears that shield her modesty from the hungry wolf-eyes of the salivating young men who compete fiercely for the honor of possessing her in their pre-booked suites in quiet hours of the early morning. Though, in truth, she had already lost that particular flower to her best friend, the Honorable Cynthia Negus, amidst the pungent scent of salt-sea breezes and coconutty yellow furze on a Brighton clifftop many months previous.

Tonight, though, the girls are in the mood for adventure and, once the speeches have been made, the dance-card obligations fulfilled and the waxy white corsages worn and wilted, they gather up a herd of young bucks and escape, speeding out along the nearly-deserted Strand and off towards the black hiss of the river in Freddie Heathcote-Willoughby's bright red roadster, laughing as the warm breeze rushes through their hair like lovers' fingers. They've already explored all the intricate petals of each other's cunts, sucked on engorged sugar-pink nipples like hard-jelly jube-jubes and thrilled to the rhythms of their own bodies as they lay gasping like iridescent fish in the blood-pumping afterglow of orgasms; and now they're ready for cock. In fact, a whole carload of it, half a gallon of the most valuable semen in London all pent up in one tiny vehicle and eager to be spilled for their pleasure.

And Lady Cynthia knows of a cinema beyond the south bank. You know the kind of place we mean. Perhaps you've even been to one. Certainly not one of the grand cathedrals of Leicester Square with their smartly uniformed usherettes and a great orchestra humming with haunting melodies; or the friendly palaces of Upper Tooting where you first laughed at stone-faced Buster Keaton or melted under Valentino's blistering gaze. No, this particular stereopticon lurks in a shady side street in Thornton Heath and boasts of no neon-lit stucco frontage or plush red velvet curtains, and its continuous performance of scratchy "imported" movies boasts of no melody save the whir of the projector and the soft moans of the patrons as they watch their unfolding erotic dreams with unabated longing.

Freddie pays for all their admission and adds a generous tip to the tired fat woman in the tiny booth by the door to ensure discretion, and then, like Alice and her rabbit burrow, they all tumble headlong into the velvet darkness within, both girls surrounded by eager young men as they take their seats and look up at the flickering images of Wonderland on the screen before them.

And it's all flesh. Naked young hopefuls from the outer fringes of the brave new Hollywoodland, pretty little things with sweet faces and stars in their big blue eyes, striking "artistic" poses on a sunset Venice Beach as the warm red wind caresses their bodies, their little breasts quivering and their nipples rubbery; then heavier older women who have already walked the mean streets and who see the film industry as the softer option, laconic in their own large-breasted nudity, rotund bellies lying unashamedly welcomingly below soft portly tits; thick hairy pussies lurking sleek and contented like fat tom cats between their milk-white thighs.

And Magda can feel the boy beside her stiffen—feel his body stance stiffen, that is, though that other thing is almost guaranteed to be stiffening too—and a thrill runs through her as she takes his hand and immediately connects to his racing pulse, getting caught up in his virulently contagious excitement as they watch the voluptuaries cavorting before them.

Then another film clunks clumsily onto the screen. Somehow opulent in its blurry sepia tone after the stark monochrome of the previous epic. But this particular burlesque is harder core and no mere girly parade. Hell, it even makes a crude attempt at a storyline.

Three girls stroll on a beach on a hot summer day, and two quickly strip off and splash in the water while the third watches, fully dressed. Then we see the mermaids laughing and beckoning to their friend to join them, but she demurely shakes her head, no, but, instead of respecting her wishes, the naked nymphs run brazenly back up the shale, buxom bottoms like white full moons, and lay hands on her, pulling the clothes from her body and quickly denuding her.

And these are no coy starlets or sweet Mary Pickford look-alikes, but strong-limbed working girls, fresh-faced farmer's daughters just off the bus from Ohio or Indiana, with heavy breasts and thick hair under their armpits. And yet Magda feels her own pussy turn to water as she watches the stocky girl (who so resembles one of her mother's kitchen maids back in their country house) have the clothing ripped from her body; groans aloud as her bra falls to the ground and her huge white tits tumble out, the nipples walnut brown and already hard, her fat cunt covered with thick blonde hair and unapologetically bestial.

"Bet you'd like to do *that* to me," she whispers mischievously into the ear of the boy beside her, her hand already on his thigh and traveling upward, heady from champagne and astounded at her own boldness as she fumbles with buttons and reaches for the thing that she has fantasized about for so long.

"Rather!" he agrees, his eager hand burrowing up her skirt in return, but she pushes him off.

"No, not yet," she breathes and wrestles with the cool cotton of his underwear, her nimble fingers quickly finding thick hair and hot flesh. "I just want to feel you while we watch …"

And, with her dainty little hand wrapped tightly around his huge thick shaft, he nods agreement, powerless to resist.

She has his cock right out now and tears her eyes away from the three naked graces on screen to sneak a peep, his member huge and standing out in front of him like a thick branch from a gnarled old tree, the soft chamois leather of his foreskin warm in her hand as she slides it up and down like the tiny plain-covered books she and Cynthia have pored-over in bed have advised, marveling at feel of him, his unyielding hardness and animal heat.

On screen the girls have started to kiss and touch each other and she knows that it's arousing him to boiling point, watching while she runs her hand slowly up and down his shaft, not rushing it or milk-machining him like some cold English Rose impatient to get to the money shot and drop the hard, beautiful thing she is holding like a hot coal; but, instead, she delights in torturing him as she drags his hood right down and denudes his slippery wet head to run a fingernail around the rim before resuming her steady up-and-down rhythm again.

"So, tell me, which of their furry little pussies do you like the best?" she giggles impishly into his ear, ogling all the cunts on the screen while squeezing his rock-hard dick mercilessly, and he mutters something incomprehensible as his whole body stiffens and then arches upwards and he comes like a volcano, all his hot white jism shooting out of him in spurt after snowy-white spurt, drenching her hand and his own pulsating cock, soaking his underwear and ruining his tuxedo.

"Now," she whispers, licking the salt off her fingers and delighting in the taste of him. "*Now*, you can squeeze my pretty little kitty and make me come ..."

------◇◇◇------

Later, they lie together on the big bed in Lady Cynthia's hotel suite, the men dispensed with and the hot night quiet. The odd snatch of conversation from watchmen on the becalmed freighters on the river floats across the rooftops and laps softly at the open French windows, and the net curtains ripple like a blush with the scant breeze; but the velvet darkness is so still that they don't quite dare to speak in anything louder than whispers.

"Men," Magda laments, almost imperceptibly. "Their cocks are so beautiful and yet they're such idiots ..." She is almost naked. The pearl dress that fifteen seamstresses labored over night and day lies in an untidy heap on the floor and she stretches her long limbs along the satin sheets of the huge bed, a flimsy pair of Parisian silk French knickers, so sheer that they show even her pale bush, and her beloved amber beads are all that separate her from total depravity.

"And what do you know of cocks, friend of mine?" Cynthia teases, taking Magda's long thin fingers in hers and pressing them to her full, lush lips, still stained a dark damson red though her lipstick has long since worn away. "Oh dear, what's this I taste? Something salty and very sexy ... My, my, has somebody been a naughty girl?"

"No naughtier than you," Magda replies, licking first one and then the other of her friend's tiny hands. "My god, Cynthia. You taste of cum on both hands. What did you do?"

"Nothing you didn't," Cynthia laughs, pulling Magda up level with her and planting a tiny kiss on her face. "Just with two of them at once ..."

"And did they make you come too?" Magda pouts, desperate to return the kiss but resisting hard, her soft blue eyes fiery with jealousy.

"No," Cynthia reassures her, laughing. "Not that they didn't try, but they just ended up more or less holding hands over my pussy. How about yours, any luck?"

And Magda laughs and remembers the boy's clumsy caress of her big prominent pudenda and the fingers that ventured in and out of her hot, wet slit without quite touching her clit. "Not a chance, I'm ravenous ..."

"Me too," the Honorable Cynthia agrees,

white spurt, drenching her hand and his own pulsating cock, soaking his underwear and ruining his tuxedo.

"Now," she whispers, licking the salt off her fingers and delighting in the taste of him. "*Now,* you can squeeze my pretty little kitty and make me come …"

◇◇◇

Later, they lie together on the big bed in Lady Cynthia's hotel suite, the men dispensed with and the hot night quiet. The odd snatch of conversation from watchmen on the becalmed freighters on the river floats across the rooftops and laps softly at the open French windows, and the net curtains ripple like a blush with the scant breeze; but the velvet darkness is so still that they don't quite dare to speak in anything louder than whispers.

"Men," Magda laments, almost imperceptibly. "Their cocks are so beautiful and yet they're such idiots …" She is almost naked. The pearl dress that fifteen seamstresses labored over night and day lies in an untidy heap on the floor and she stretches her long limbs along the satin sheets of the huge bed, a flimsy pair of Parisian silk French knickers, so sheer that they show even her pale bush, and her beloved amber beads are all that separate her from total depravity.

"And what do you know of cocks, friend of mine?" Cynthia teases, taking Magda's long thin fingers in hers and pressing them to her full, lush lips, still stained a dark damson red though her lipstick has long since worn away. "Oh dear, what's this I taste? Something salty and very sexy ... My, my, has somebody been a naughty girl?"

"No naughtier than you," Magda replies, licking first one and then the other of her friend's tiny hands. "My god, Cynthia. You taste of cum on both hands. What did you do?"

"Nothing you didn't," Cynthia laughs, pulling Magda up level with her and planting a tiny kiss on her face. "Just with two of them at once ..."

"And did they make you come too?" Magda pouts, desperate to return the kiss but resisting hard, her soft blue eyes fiery with jealousy.

"No," Cynthia reassures her, laughing. "Not that they didn't try, but they just ended up more or less holding hands over my pussy. How about yours, any luck?"

And Magda laughs and remembers the boy's clumsy caress of her big prominent pudenda and the fingers that ventured in and out of her hot, wet slit without quite touching her clit. "Not a chance, I'm ravenous ..."

"Me too," the Honorable Cynthia agrees,

kissing her again. "Want to see what's on the menu?" Like Magda's, her dress lies abandoned on the snowy polar-bearskin rug and she lies on the bed in a tiny chemise and nude-colored silk stockings with garters like tiny rosebuds. No evidence of a bra or panties.

And Magda returns the kiss this time as the two of them slowly melt into each other's arms, and she feels her nipples become as hard as the cinema boy's cock as Cynthia runs her fingers over them.

"Strip me," Magda moans when they finally break for air and Cynthia laughs.

"You're only wearing your ..."

"I know, pull them down. No, not like that, jerk them off roughly like a boy would!"

"Like this?"

"Oh yes, just like that. Now squeeze my pussy like you've never touched one before ..."

"*Oh, gosh, I say, old girl,*" Cynthia mimics. "*You're all furry, I didn't know girls had hair down there!*"

"Silly boy, not *all* girls have it," Magda replies, joining the game and rubbing herself frantically on her friend's hand. "Only the special ones who turn into animals in the dead of night and come to eat you up ..."

"Then it's just about time that we both did some eating," Cynthia whispers in her own voice, pulling her slip off over her head and slithering down Magda's naked body like a pole dancer. She's a little smaller that Magda but her breasts are considerably larger, with dark brown nipples and huge areolas the size of half-crowns, a tight waist and short shapely legs. But it's her cute little cunt that has caught your eye, isn't it, with its downy neatly-trimmed bush a beautiful golden brown with a little fleck of white blonde up the center, and fleshy pink petals peeping like shy maids from her deep, deep slit.

And normally they kiss and tease for hours before they finally let tongues and fingers finish the job, but tonight they've been kept on the boil for too long and all they crave is fulfillment.

"Don't kiss me, finger fuck me, hard and clumsy like a man would do!" Cynthia commands, pushing deep into Magda's crevice as she speaks and brushing against her stiff clit in passing.

"Like this?"

"Yes, that's good. But hard. Harder. Rub my clitty with your thumb …"

"Oh god, Cynthia, I'm desperate to come. Do it properly …"

"No, rub yourself up against my fingers like I'm doing to you!"

"I think I'll wet myself if I try to come like this …"

"Promises, promises …"

"Oh fuck … I think I'm coming anyway … oh yes, I'm coming. I'm coming, I'm coming …"

"Me too, don't stop, oh fuck, fuck, fuck, I love you more than anyone in the world. Even being a man you thrill my clit so beautifully …"

And normally they lie in each other's arms, luxuriating in the afterglow, their bodies awash with sensations, skin gently tingling, eyelids gradually getting heavier as sleep eventually overcomes them; but tonight Magda experiences a new restlessness, an itch that demands to be scratched and won't acknowledge satiation.

Cynthia is boneless, like a rubber doll that can be bent to any shape, and Magda clambers on top of her and starts to rub her cunt up and down the cool flesh of her friend's opal-white thigh, not gently, but like a she-wolf in heat, desperate for relief.

"I need to be fucked," she pleads urgently, bending down to plant hard kisses on Cynthia's long swan neck, biting with frustration and leaving lover's marks, her crotch still bumping and grinding below. "I love you with all my heart, Cynthia, but I do so wish you had a cock …"

And Cynthia laughs a sad, bittersweet laugh

and pushes her friend gently off and rises, a naked fairy thing in the silver moonlight, and goes to find her bags amidst the heaps of discarded clothing on their hotel room floor.

Magda watches her keenly and groans aloud as Cynthia bends down. "What are you doing, lover? Aside from showing me your delicious little white ass, that is ..."

"Getting you a cock," Cynthia replies enigmatically, taking something wrapped in an anonymous black velvet bag from her suitcase. "I knew this day would eventually come and so I asked the Toy Maker of Paris if he could help, and he hasn't let me down. Look ..."

And Cynthia turns and stands before her, pale and naked in the moonlight, except that she isn't the old Cynthia any more. She is still as beautiful, still as alabaster white, still the same fine-looking tits with their huge brown nipples like coconut mushroom stalks, still the same sexy legs and creamy thighs. But there, there where Magda's eyes naturally rivet, there where Cynthia's foxy little bush should be neatly nestled, sits a big, fat sleepy cock, thick and heavy and thinking about getting hard. Not a man's cock but Cynthia's cock, hot and horny, and getting itself ready to give Magda the fucking she's always been dreaming about. Here, now, tonight ...

"Cynthia, what have you done?" Magda asks in a breathless whisper, eyes riveted to the big semi-flaccid organ, her breathing rapid and labored like Red Riding Hood finding a Wolf in her Grandma's bed.

"Don't worry, it's only clockwork," her friend replies, coming so close that Magda can almost reach out and touch the thick and menacing beast that nestles between her legs. "The Toy Maker made it for me, it's fashioned from gold inside and has a precision mechanism designed by Swiss watchmakers. Come, don't be afraid, touch it, it's connected to my clit and it'll rise up if you stroke it, plus it'll drive me wild …"

And Magda is afraid and aroused all at once, and she really doesn't want to go anywhere near that frightening, alluring thing. But she's in the grip of a primordial force that is older than time itself and she's powerless to resist it, and, as though in some misty erotic dream, she sees her own tiny hand slowly reach out and tentatively stroke the huge prick that sits like a phallic cuckoo in the nest of Cynthia's soft and hairy bush, and, sure enough, with an imperceptible whir of hidden cogwheels, the behemoth rises up and stiffens in her palm.

And Cynthia lets out a soft moan and pulls her close. "That's right, feel me, squeeze me, make me really stiff and hard for you so I can fuck you like you deserve to be fucked. Oh yes, that feels so good. It's amazing, it's like it's an extension of my own body. Like I've got a huge hard clitoris sticking out in front of me and I'm going to fuck you with it."

"Oh Cynthia, would you? Would you please?" Magda moans, one hand still gripping the big, ever-stiffening phallus, the other frantically stroking Cynthia's firm tennis-girl's belly and cupping her big quivering tits with their hard rubber nipples. "Would you fuck me with your big stiff prick, hard and heavy, like there's no tomorrow?"

And in reply Cynthia pushes her friend onto the huge bed and gently parts her legs, her hands everywhere as the two girls kiss passionately, tongues deep inside each other's mouths, Cynthia's hands on Magda's inner thighs, up and down, up and down, getting closer and closer to heaven, finally unable to resist and cupping Magda's big prominent mound and sliding her fingers inside.

"Not your fingers, use your cock," Magda begs, her nails clawing at Cynthia's flawless back, and the other girl smiles and then, softly, firmly, guides the monster in, Magda's cunt hot and slippery like greased velvet, taking the huge throbbing member with ease, inch after inch, inch after inch, until it's right up there, a separate vibrating mechanism kicking-in and whirring softly against Magda's huge and swollen clit as Cynthia thrusts and thrusts again.

"Harder," Magda moans. Begs. Commands. And Cynthia obliges.

"Like this?"

"No harder!"

"How about this?"

"Oh yes, much better. Now keep doing that and kiss me …"

"This is amazing," Cynthia gasps, her thick honey-blond hair wet with sweat. "But I think I'm going to come soon. Are you close enough to come with me?"

"Of course. We've always come in unison before, this isn't going to be any different …"

"Then get ready to come … *now*," Cynthia breathes as she thrusts hard and fast, pummeling into Magda's pussy like there is no tomorrow, the big mechanical cock between her legs tightening and tightening until it detects Magda's orgasm and gives Cynthia the release that she's been craving, with what feels like gallon after gallon of thick white semen substitute shooting out of her and filling her friend's cunt up and overflowing onto the crumpled satin sheets of the best suite in the Savoy …

Chapter Three
Chlotilde and the Toy Maker

She remembers the hospital, and how the bright sun hurt her eyes when she lifted the blind on the window in her room, wincing as the surgical steel brightness of the post holocaust skies seared her retina. *Here, you'll need these*, the armed Patrician assigned to her ward had said matter-of-factly, handing her the military-issue green visor that she still uses to this day, *the sky's too bright for the naked eye any more.*

And, though the rest is pretty blank, she can also remember going out for the first time, the dry air and the sensation of the hot tar melting under her boots, crisscross diamonds of cracking mud along the dried-up bed of the Seine, and the strange new fashions being sported along the boulevards in an austere world which had suddenly found itself bereft of men.

But today all that is in the past and Magda is out on a new mission, striding along the *Champs Élysée* and ignoring the Demimonde—fey Damsels who wear their hair long and piled high upon their heads, with heavily padded Victorianesque bodices and hobble skirts split up to the thigh; and Dandies, in neat khaki trouser suits, their hair cut short beneath their impenetrable sun goggles and topped with neat trilbies. A summons is nestled firmly in Magda's gold brocade waistcoat pocket, directing her to report to the legendary Toy Maker at his residence in the now-derelict glasshouses of the *Jardin des Plantes,*.

And she smiles softly to herself at the mention of that name, remembering a hot summer night at the Savoy and Cynthia Negus standing over her with her large mechanical cock …

The Toy Maker is a robust male of about sixty with short-cropped white hair and a dark, outdoor worker's tan. He's lean and neatly dressed, sitting straight-backed and assertive in a glittering steel wheelchair. He'd be tall if he were to stand, not at all the disheveled eccentric that Magda has been expecting, and she feels a momentary shiver of excitement as, already unused to the presence of men, she takes in his virile demeanor and searing gray eyes. Even his comforting scent, a heady blend of fresh air and aromatic tobacco, seems laced with pheromones and she finds herself conjecturing about how that lean cat-like body will look when stripped of all its expertly-tailored outer clothing.

And they are meeting in the seared outer garden of the semi-derelict Equatorial Palace, the huge botanical glass dome cracked and bent out of shape, all the magnificent exterior shrubs and trees wilted and shriveled from the white heat of the cloudless sky.

"They've given me this place to live and work," the authoritative man says brusquely, one muscular arm propelling his chair into the inner gloom of the shattered glass palace. "Everyone's a bit afraid of it, I think. Too much greenery. People just can't seem to cope with vegetation any more. Mind your step now, it takes a while to get used to the light and the humidity."

And, inside, though the sun still streams viciously through the huge green-tinted panels of the decayed arboretum, the air is soft and humid like some half-remembered tropical jungle, and living trees form a lofty cathedral-like arch above their heads, lush creepers and verdant vines trailing downwards as the steamy atmosphere caresses Magda's face with hot wet fingers.

The Toy Maker turns in his chair and smiles at her. "It gives you quite a jolt, doesn't it?"

And Magda nods wordlessly, eyes wide, and points up at a flock of brightly colored parakeets on a high branch. "Birds too?"

"Oh no," the tall man laughs. "They're not real. Just some of my old automatons. Like Jet here, he's my pride and joy ..."

And Magda tries not to cry out as a large black panther snakes silently out of the undergrowth and brushes past her, its feet swishing thorough the soft green ground cover of shy Touch-Me-Not plants, their tender leaves closing like a field of sea anemones in its wake.

"The beast, it's an automation? He's so real ..."

"Yes, he's very advanced, isn't he," the Toy Maker says proudly, scratching the creature's great head and making its voice box purr. "But come, here are my living quarters. Let us go inside and conduct our business before Chlotilde brings us tea. You're no doubt anxious to discover why you're *really* here ..."

The panther glides silently in behind them, its huge black paws quiet as a mouse, only the faintest whirr of cogwheels discernible from the inner clockwork that propels its sinewy skeleton forward.

"What is … *was* this place?" Magda asks, still wide-eyed and looking all around her, her boots making a hollow tap-tap-tap sound on the cracked black and white checkered marble floor.

"A tea dance ballroom within the garden, I believe," the Toy Maker says disinterestedly, sweeping across the floor like a wheelchair-bound Valentino. "Now, hurry along, sit yourself down and I'll tell you what's what. Oh, here's Chlotilde with tea. You do like tea, don't you? Please don't say that you don't. It upsets her terribly when they don't know what it is …"

And Magda looks at him blankly as she searches for some suitable reply, but he's not listening anyway, so she sits meekly down in an old gilded wicker chair that has once graced the big palm room when it echoed to the mellow sounds of Geraldo, and elegant ladies had danced together to while away the long hot Parisian afternoons.

"Tea, you take it black with a lemon slice, or at least that's how you used to in the old life," a deep female voice says in her ear, and Magda looks up to see a broad-shouldered provincial woman of around forty, clad, not in current Dandy attire, but tough worker's trousers and an old striped Breton jersey, her military sun goggles slung carelessly around her neck like a scarf.

"Yes, thank you, I did ... *do*," she says and the big woman beams.

"And you'll have cake too. *Clafoutis de cerise*. I made it myself ..."

And Magda gasps with a heady feeling of long-forgotten decadence as the panther rubs its head against her thigh and Chlotilde deftly cuts a thin slice from the moist pastry, flipping it expertly onto an old plate made from a china so fine that it is almost transparent, fat black cherries oozing languidly from what Magda already knows will be a faultless custard.

"My Grandmamma, she always soaked the cherries in kirsch ..." she begins, a faraway look in her eyes, taking the plate and the petite gold plated pastry fork from the woman's large, almost masculine, hand.

"*Mais oui*, of course," Chlotilde replies. "I too!"

"But where do you find kirsch in this day and age? Or cherries for that matter, the wineries are all destroyed and the orchards and vineyards devastated ..."

"Oh, I have my ways," Chlotilde says, tapping the side of her nose and winking at Magda.

"Oh, do be quiet, Chlotilde," the Toy Maker butts in rudely. "She doesn't care about your bootleg liquor-makers, she's just being polite. Now, Magda, eat your blasted cake and listen to me. The Party has summoned you here because you entered into the

State Lottery and have been selected as our chosen candidate to be a mother to the next generation. The Pioneer Generation they're calling it, in their infinite wisdom. Now, as you know, there are not many fertile males remaining since the Pestilences, and procreation is vital if we are to survive. Therefore, if you will consent to bear my heir, your prize is that you may live here and raise our child without having to perform further labor. And, though I am not a young man I am still fertile, and your intelligence scores almost match those of my own, making us a perfect breeding unit …"

"And I would have to … *make love with you?*" Magda interrupts, half aroused, half horrified.

"Ah, the wheelchair …" he says, a little sadly. "Yes, some degree of intimacy between us would be required, but this would *not* be a marriage. Sexual contact would be solely for the purpose of impregnating you. Now, I am a man of initiative and not debate. Time is off the essence. Our data says that you are at the peak of your fertility cycle today, and it is therefore essential that we act immediately. So, Magda, what do you say. Will you perform your patriotic duty to the Party and be a mother to a Pioneer?"

And, with an odd, half-remembered sensation like a caged bird fluttering frantically in her ribcage, she slowly nods, her face flaming and her cunt beginning to pulsate.

"Yes, Sir, I consent," she says in a small voice. "You may do with me as you will, I will not resist …"

They have given her the Room of Windows, an old viewing gallery set, like an eyrie, high above the Palm House and at the apex of the glass dome of the semi-derelict palace, the lights of Paris spread out all around her like spilled gemstones on a vast black velvet cloak. Chlotilde has undressed her and drawn her a bath, and she luxuriates now in the scented foam, watching the older woman as she potters to and fro in the flickering candlelight.

"What he said, about me not caring about your cookery. It wasn't true. I wanted you to know that," she says suddenly, reaching her small wet hand from the large circular tub and taking Chlotilde's big work-hardened fingers in her own.

"I know, Cherie," the other woman says softly, not quite meeting her eye. "But you must not worry, I am used to him and his petty temper tantrums."

"Then we are friends? I could not bear to live here if we were not on good terms …"

Her voice trails off as Chlotilde utters a small noncommittal grunt and makes to turn her back, but

Magda holds her firmly. "If we are truly friends, you will help me, Chlotilde?"

"What do you require?"

"To be, you know, *intimate*, with him, well, the thought of it partly excites me, but it also makes me afraid. Will you help me prepare myself for him?"

"Prepare yourself how?" Chlotilde asks, looking at her half quizzically, half with interest.

"Like this ..." Magda replies bluntly, taking the other's rough hand and squeezing it to her bare breast, her fine athletic body slippery with scented bath oils.

"Ah, *this* I can help you with," Chlotilde purrs, her fingers surprisingly nimble for their size, cupping Magda's tits and quickly bringing the nipples up springy and hard.

"But you must not let me come," the girl breathes, her whole body already shaking. "I merely want to be as slippery as sea-stroked rocks after the tide has departed when I go to him ..."

"And you doubt his ability to instill such a reaction in you? *Pourquoi?* I assure you, I assist him with his ablutions and have seen his body. He is a fine specimen and will not disappoint you."

"Yes, but he is, by his own admission, an impatient man," Magda pants as Chlotilde's big hands slide under the foamy water and start to caress her lower belly and inner thighs. "I fear that he will not waste much time seeking to arouse me, and I would like to be ready to receive him when he wants me …"

Chlotilde laughs kindly as her hands find soft and secret places. "You went with men in the old life? Or solely with women?"

"I liked both," Magda breathes softly as the other's fingers enter her, gently but insistently, pushing deep inside her, then slide back out and start to circle round and round her clit in ever closing rings.

"You like?"

"I like. Kiss me …"

And the older woman hesitates but Magda is adamant and pulls them together, and their lips suddenly join as if they have been molded to interlock with each other, tongues gently dueling, not invading or pushing in, but delighting in the sensation of each other, hearts beating in unison, pussies turning to water …

And Magda is on the brink of coming as Chlotilde abruptly breaks their embrace and backs quickly away, standing flattened against the glass, breathing heavily and with a strange haunted look in her eyes, her whole body shaking with desire.

The Toy Maker has been lifted from his chair

and reclines on a low dais in the center of the old dance floor, two elaborate candelabras dripping ruby-red wax behind him and the big animatronic panther stretched out at his feet on the cold black and white marble.

He is completely naked and his body is powerful and sinewy in the soft light, his arms, legs, chest and abdomen covered in thick white hair like a snow wolf, his long thin cock standing up like the sole lightning-blasted tree on a barren heath, his cynical eyes watchful and alert.

"I please you?" he asks quietly and Magda nods, her heart thumping and her cunt desperate for fulfillment.

"Then Chlotilde may disrobe you?"

She nods again. She has dressed for the occasion, not in an old-world gown, but her best suede-lapelled Dandy suit in a soft moss green worsted with an antique frilled-front tuxedo shirt beneath, half tucked in to the waistband of her pants, half out and gleaming white in the flickering light. But she has left her boots in her room and stands barefoot before him, delighting in the chill of the cold marble beneath her as Chlotilde's big fingers gently undo the buttons on her trousers and help her to step out of them.

And her bare cunt is still as magnificent as it was on that day atop the Brighton cliff when Cynthia

Negus had first inched her silky panties down and gasped aloud at her loveliness, run her hand through the thick clump of cornflower yellow hair and slipped her curious fingers inside and claimed her maidenhood. And today even the urbane Toy Maker tries not to swallow as he beholds her long tapering legs and proud pussy, but is betrayed by his long wolverine cock which twitches like an eager tup in the presence of her fecund nakedness.

"Remove everything else except her brassiere," he coughs and gruffly instructs Chlotilde who willingly obliges. "Then bring her to me ..."

She wants to go down on him straight away, take that huge bare head, already glistening with glassy drops of pre-cum, and suck him till he begs for mercy, but he's fearful of wasting any of his seed and won't permit it, so she has to satisfy herself with merely touching and a little squeezing, reacquainting herself with the feel and scent of real cock before he enters her.

"You visit automation houses?" he asks in a tight voice, a voice she recognizes as that of a man trying hard not to come too quickly, and so she nods, yes.

"Which?"

"Madame Augustine ..."

"Ah, my early prototypes, they satisfy you?"

She pauses in her ministration to his cock, deliberately pulling his foreskin down as far as it will stretch and keeping it there, squeezing him just gently enough to make more pearls of clear liquid form around the little eye-shaped slit in the fiery-red head.

"Satisfy me? No, they are cold and unfeeling machines, how could they satisfy me? But they scratch the itch and make the longings go away, for a while, at any rate ..."

He nods, more to himself than to her, as if making a mental note.

"But, come," Magda says, climbing onto him. "Enough talk, I need you inside me ..."

"It is not good for conception this way ..." he starts to protest but she silences him by taking hold of his prick and guiding it gently into herself as she lowers her pussy down onto his hardness, and he gasps as he feels her wetness and heat.

"Good?" she asks, beginning to ease herself slowly up and down and he nods breathlessly.

"Then let me fuck you in earnest," she gasps, lifting her tight buttocks into the air and then slamming down on him again, her big slippery cunt sliding up and down his erection, up and down, like the great pistons on the city generation plant. "Fuck, your cock is amazing. When we're done, I want to take it in my ass ... feel you going right up my tight little back hole and really stretching me till I come ..."

He lets out a moan and, with a manful effort, just manages to stop himself from shooting his load, then he pushes her gently off him, his dick sliding out and lying on his tight belly, all slick and slippery from her pussy juices.

"Did I do something wrong?" she asks, but he shakes his head.

"No, you did everything right," he pants, gasping, lying her down and turning onto his side. "Too right, in fact. Chlotilde, come, assist me, I need to mount her properly for procreation ..."

"Ah, such a romantic," Chlotilde smiles, lifting him into the place he wants to be, though all the while her eyes are busy eating up Magda's nakedness. "There, you are in position, treat her well ..." And she makes to step out of the circle of candlelight but the girl stops her and takes her hand.

"Stay," she whispers as the Toy Maker nudges his long thin cock inside her and begins to thrust, hard, and Chlotilde nods.

"I am here, but you must hold him," she instructs, letting go of the girl's hand, and Magda nods and grips the Toy Maker's tight buns and pulls him towards her, trying to meet his lips but finding that he evades her as he plows mercilessly into her.

"I'm so close," he begs, thrusting hard and fast. "Tip me over, make me come …"

And she nods again, remembering a secret from the little beige books she read in the life before, and slides one hand into his asscrack, quickly finding his anus and stroking it, then deftly worming a finger inside and pushing hard, feeling his heat as he slams into her with a yell, his hot white semen shooting hard and fast into her as she claws at him mercilessly with her free hand.

Chapter Four

The Cherry Orchard

She lies breathing shallowly in the big bed in the Room of Windows, naked and alone, a sleepless princess in her ivory tower with all the lights of Paris spread out around her like phosphorescent gem stones in the silky dark.

She has not come, the Toy Maker having rolled off her as soon as his seed was spent, shouting bad-temperedly for Chlotilde to come and help him up, and Magda had crept away, angry and humiliated, clutching her clothes to her front, back up the long winding staircase to her room, her whole body shaking and her knees weak, desperate to climax and knowing that manual stimulation will give her no respite.

And she wants to blame the Toy Maker, heap

abuse on his head for his lack of human decency and, oh especially this, his inability to satisfy a woman. And yet ... And yet a little voice in her head reminds her that this was not to be a marriage, and sex between them would be solely for the purposes of procreation. And that there was never any mention of her satisfaction in their bargain, and she doubted if the Party had ever even considered it.

Clenching her fists she wonders if she should try to sleep. Then she wonders if she should pace the floor. Or drag the plump and silky bolster up and down between her thighs like a saw horse until she finally comes, or ... And then she hears the unmistakable sound of soft footfalls on the long iron stairs that lead to her bedchamber.

"Who goes there?" she calls melodramatically down to the darkness, knowing the answer already.

"Only one who loves you," comes the reply in that familiar voice. "One who has come to finish what she started."

"That may be hard, for I am in need of much satisfaction ..." Magda begins, but the other cuts her short.

"The Toy Maker sleeps soundlessly down below and we have all night! To kiss and touch and leisurely explore ..."

And then Chlotilde is in her arms and their lips

meet, furiously, hungrily. Aching for each other. Hands everywhere, bodies pushing desperately against each other, Magda's hungry cunt rubbing urgently against the coarse fabric of Chlotilde's rough worker's trousers.

"Strip me, bare my skin so that I can hold you naked," the tall woman eventually begs, and Magda doesn't hesitate to oblige. It's only a matter of seconds to pull off the striped sweater and unfasten the jeans, and she has Chlotilde stripped down to her corset within a minute.

"My, my! Did somebody wear this for me?" she asks coquettishly, running inquisitive hands up and down the whalebone and silk, frantic fingers fumbling furiously for the fasteners.

"I did indeed," Chlotilde agrees, her breathing ragged. "And I'm not wearing anything underneath …"

And Magda groans as she investigates, lets out an oh so soft moan when she finds warm cat-like fur and slippery wetness.

"Oh, I'm going to eat you …"

"Strip me first, I want you to see me naked before you fuck me!"

But Magda's skillful fingers have already unlaced the silky basque and the bulky garment slips soundlessly to the ground, revealing a body that is like a lost continent of ice in the silver moonlight that streams eerily through the windows.

Chlotilde is a big woman with heavy hips and broad shoulders and her body is a moonlit arctic expanse, her huge breasts rising and falling, her dark brown nipples already hard and rubbery like glacé fruit, her hips and thighs like frost-kissed alabaster, her cunt an enchanted forest covered in a dense undergrowth of thick dark hair that looks coarse but feels like silk when Magda strokes it.

"I know you are impatient to climax but, please, kiss me again first," Chlotilde begs, taking Magda into her arms, their breasts rubbing gently together as they embrace naked for the first time, skin to skin, made for each other.

But Magda's impatience has melted like snowflakes on a wet pavement, and she takes her lover gently into her arms, luxuriating in their shared intimacy. "We have all night, beloved, so you may kiss me as much as you like …"

"Oh, I shall, and for every night to come if you will let me."

"Don't talk anymore. Just kiss …"

And a cautious dawn caresses the edge of the horizon, threatening to turn the whole sky into a raging conflagration at any moment, when they finally acknowledge satisfaction and lie back, exhausted, on the big bed.

Magda is all for falling quickly to sleep before the ferocious sun floods the glass room and makes it uninhabitable until dusk, but Chlotilde seems to want to talk, and sits up, her big naked body like an iceberg amidst the turbulent sea of rumpled bed linen, her opalescent skin practically glowing in the early morning light.

"I know it is too early to speak of love," she whispers. "But there are decisions which must be made in haste, and such as you or I have not the luxury of time in which to make them. So, I beg of you. Could you love me?"

And Magda remembers the heat of their embraces, the way that Chlotilde holds her, the fact that they have both come together again and again, their cunts pulsating in absolute harmony as if they have once been joined and still function as one being. And she nods. "Yes, I could love you. In fact, I think that I maybe already love you just a little bit …"

And Chlotilde swallows and looks, for a moment, like a woman trying to decide whether to jump from a roof or not, and then, with a heartfelt sigh, she makes her decision and plunges.

"The Toy Maker, he has lied to you," she

begins. "There is no lottery and there have been many women here before you and many will come after. And there will be no reward, no life free of labor spent happily bringing up your child. They will test you in a day or so, and if you prove positive you will be transferred immediately to a breeding unit in England until you give birth. Then they will take the child into the Pioneer Program and you will never see it again. Just as you will never see this house or that man. And I do not yet know where they send the mothers once the children are born. There are many, many conflicting stories, but the best of what has been whispered to me is that you will be sent back to your place of work alone."

She pauses for breath, and then continues.

"But I can offer you a different life. You, me and the child. You have tasted the food that I cook so you know that there are other lands, lands beyond the great mountain ranges and the Contagion Barriers where the sky is not on fire and the trees still grow, and I know that they exist because I have met the people who steal out from them to sell their wares and I have seen the fruit from them in my own hands. And though I do not know how to get there I have studied your papers and I know that you are a cartographer, and that you know all the forbidden maps like the palms of your own hands, and that you could guide us over the mountains …"

"I *could* do that," Magda interrupts, her heart pounding. "But what of the patrols?"

"I have his papers, his identity discs and a handful of his credits. If we disable his wheelchair while he sleeps he will be stranded here alone and it will take him days to summon assistance, time enough for us to be clear of the city and the great airships with their watchful eyes. But our time runs short and already the sun rises and is burning off the clouds, so what do you say, my best beloved, will you come with me on this journey and learn to love me as I already love you?"

And there is a long silence as the bright sun pulsates from the east and the bent iron frame of the old building starts to creak with the heat of a new day.

"In my dreams I am always in a cherry orchard," Magda eventually replies. "But I continuously see it as a place that can be both of love or heartache …"

"Ah, that describes all of life, Cherie," Chlotilde says sadly, planting a soft kiss on Magda's hair. "But, hurry, he stirs in his bed. We must decide. Will you come with me?"

And Magda slowly nods. A nod that says yes, yes I will come with you. And I know that it will not be easy, and that we may die in the process of this perilous journey down the beanstalk and away from this enchanted castle in the clouds. But I am willing to take a risk on you, lover of mine, because maybe, *just maybe*, if luck remains firmly on our side, we *might* just manage to live happily-ever-after after all.

And it is a beautifully heartfelt speech, but, in the hurry of a decision desperate to be made and a sleeping giant stirring down below, all the pretty words remain unsaid, and, aloud, the only thing she whispers is: "Get dressed, my darling, we have a long road ahead of us!"

But it is enough for Chlotilde …

Also available from Sweetmeats Press
Various Authors
ATHLETIC AESTHETIC

Athletic Aesthetic celebrates the sensuality of sport in this collection of five erotic tales. Athletes and spectators alike refuse to settle for second-best, as tenacious desire and expert technique always make for a perfect finish. Whether you're at the 18th hole, or the bottom of the ninth, always play to win!

"A standout title." – *Library Journal*

Rigorous Training by *Lisa Fox* – Christy Turner is close to making the U.S. Gymnastics Team. If she can convince a reclusive trainer to help her, she might just be able to find the edge that she needs.

Doubleheader by *Emerald* – Caught between two heavy-hitting baseball players, a team boss must consider her position very carefully when both players come to play for her.

Monocoque by *Vanessa Wu* – A chance meeting on a plane helps a young businesswoman understand the finer nuances of Formula One motor racing.

Playing with the Big Boys by *Lexie Bay* – In her bid to climb the corporate ladder, a determined sales executive uses golf to make sure her own needs are met!

The Master by *Malin James*

A top-level fencer must compete for a chance to train with The Master. The days will be long, and the training will be hard ... but just who is The Master?

Also available from Sweetmeats Press

Various Authors
WANDERLUST

Wanderlust is a portmanteau of erotic stories about travel, exploration and discovery. It is said that travel broadens the mind, quickens the pulse, and heightens the libido. So let the stories within these pages take you away!

"Black sweeps readers away with five astonishing tales of women on the move" – *Publishers Weekly*

The Passenger by *Annabeth Leong* – Suzanne is trying to escape her small town. But when she climbs aboard a truck full of captivating curiosities, she soon discovers she's not the only one trying to escape…

Packing Steel by *Lana Fox* – A jaded hitwoman is called out for one last job. But will she be able to make the hit if she falls in love with the mark?

Love Gun by *Fulani* – A traffic jam introduces Cerise to a steampunk craftsman. Turns out, he's recently made a Love Gun; and Cerise dares him to use it on her …

Going Up by *Lily Harlem* – Faye has got herself a new man who takes great pleasure in introducing her to new experiences. A hot air balloon ride over the English countryside is only the start!

Heat by *Stella Harris* – A woman joins a volunteer group in Haiti. In the intense heat of the tropics, she lets down her barriers and discovers a lot more about herself.

Also available from Sweetmeats Press

Janine Ashbless
FIERCE ENCHANTMENTS

Fierce Enchantments is a collection of ten short stories full of fantasy, magic and lust. Against the darkest and most perilous backgrounds, the blaze of desire burns even brighter. Erotica at its fiercest and most breathtaking! This book is part of Janine Ashbless' Enchantment collection, which includes Cruel Enchantment and Dark Enchantment.

"Fierce Enchantments is a vivid and diverse mixture of tales: kinky vampire hunters here, a re-imagining of ancient China there, a session of filthy fun in Camelot and much, much more." – *Amazon*

"The best erotic fairy tale writer around," – *Saskia Walker*

"How one writer can produce story after story to such a very high standard is awesome—she puts other writers to shame. There are not enough superlatives to describe how I felt" – *Jade: the International Erotic Art and Literature Magazine*

Also available from Sweetmeats Press

Kyoko Church
DIARY OF A LIBRARY NERD

That's what this will be. A safe haven.
A place for no holds barred ranting.
A place for secrets. And drawing. Even if it's bad. Even if it's wrong.
No one will see here. No one will see this.
This is just for me.

Charlotte has secrets.

Charlotte Campbell no longer recognizes her life. Once a shy, married librarian, she now finds herself jilted, holed up in her deceased father's run down cottage, and demoted to working in "The Dungeon" with only an automated book sorter for company. Then there's the drawings she does. They are not what her work colleagues might expect. And there's Nathan, a young patron at the library—the reason for her demotion and the inspiration for her art.

When Nathan's emails reveal a startling truth, Charlotte discovers a new dimension of her sexuality. But unsettling dreams from her past continue to plague her and Charlotte is eventually forced to confront her most deeply rooted fears.

Part Bridget Jones' Diary and part Story of O, Diary of a Library Nerd is the Wimpy Kid for adults. Compelling, erotic and accompanied by the drawings from Charlotte Campbell's very grown-up mind, this private memoir of exploration and discovery is not to be missed!

CPSIA information can be obtained at www.ICGtesting.com
Printed in the USA
LVOW10s0519151215

466595LV00013B/29/P